TO CATCH A KILLER

DI SAM COBBS

BOOK ELEVEN

M A COMLEY

Thank you once again to Clive Rowlandson for allowing me to use one of his stunning photos for the cover.

Also a massive thank you to all the staff at The Gather, my second home, who have shown me nothing but kindness since losing my dear mother.

ALSO BY M A COMLEY

Blind Justice (Novella)

Cruel Justice (Book #1)

Mortal Justice (Novella)

Impeding Justice (Book #2)

Final Justice (Book #3)

Foul Justice (Book #4)

Guaranteed Justice (Book #5)

Ultimate Justice (Book #6)

Virtual Justice (Book #7)

Hostile Justice (Book #8)

Tortured Justice (Book #9)

Rough Justice (Book #10)

Dubious Justice (Book #11)

Calculated Justice (Book #12)

Twisted Justice (Book #13)

Justice at Christmas (Short Story)

Prime Justice (Book #14)

Heroic Justice (Book #15)

Shameful Justice (Book #16)

Immoral Justice (Book #17)

Toxic Justice (Book #18)

Overdue Justice (Book #19)

Unfair Justice (a 10,000 word short story)

Irrational Justice (a 10,000 word short story)

Seeking Justice (a 15,000 word novella)

Caring For Justice (a 24,000 word novella)

Savage Justice (a 17,000 word novella)

Justice at Christmas #2 (a 15,000 word novella)

Gone in Seconds (Justice Again series #1)

Ultimate Dilemma (Justice Again series #2)

Shot of Silence (Justice Again series #3)

Taste of Fury (Justice Again series #4)

Crying Shame (Justice Again series #5)

See No Evil (Justice Again #6)

To Die For (DI Sam Cobbs #1)

To Silence Them (DI Sam Cobbs #2)

To Make Them Pay (DI Sam Cobbs #3)

To Prove Fatal (DI Sam Cobbs #4)

To Condemn Them (DI Sam Cobbs #5)

To Punish Them (DI Sam Cobbs #6)

To Entice Them (DI Sam Cobbs #7)

To Control Them (DI Sam Cobbs #8)

To Endanger Lives (DI Sam Cobbs #9)

To Hold Responsible (DI Sam Cobbs #10)

To Catch a Killer (DI Sam Cobbs #11)

Forever Watching You (DI Miranda Carr thriller)

Wrong Place (DI Sally Parker thriller #1)

No Hiding Place (DI Sally Parker thriller #2)

Cold Case (DI Sally Parker thriller#3)

Deadly Encounter (DI Sally Parker thriller #4)

Lost Innocence (DI Sally Parker thriller #5)

Goodbye My Precious Child (DI Sally Parker #6)

The Missing Wife (DI Sally Parker #7)

Truth or Dare (DI Sally Parker #8)

Where Did She Go? (DI Sally Parker #9)

Sinner (DI Sally Parker #10)

Web of Deceit (DI Sally Parker Novella)

The Missing Children (DI Kayli Bright #1)

Killer On The Run (DI Kayli Bright #2)

Hidden Agenda (DI Kayli Bright #3)

Murderous Betrayal (Kayli Bright #4)

Dying Breath (Kayli Bright #5)

Taken (DI Kayli Bright #6)

The Hostage Takers (DI Kayli Bright Novella)

No Right to Kill (DI Sara Ramsey #1)

Killer Blow (DI Sara Ramsey #2)

The Dead Can't Speak (DI Sara Ramsey #3)

Deluded (DI Sara Ramsey #4)

The Murder Pact (DI Sara Ramsey #5)

Twisted Revenge (DI Sara Ramsey #6)

The Lies She Told (DI Sara Ramsey #7)

For The Love Of… (DI Sara Ramsey #8)

Run for Your Life (DI Sara Ramsey #9)

Cold Mercy (DI Sara Ramsey #10)

Sign of Evil (DI Sara Ramsey #11)

Indefensible (DI Sara Ramsey #12)

Locked Away (DI Sara Ramsey #13)

I Can See You (DI Sara Ramsey #14)

The Kill List (DI Sara Ramsey #15)

Crossing The Line (DI Sara Ramsey #16)

Time to Kill (DI Sara Ramsey #17)

Deadly Passion (DI Sara Ramsey #18)

Son Of The Dead (DI Sara Ramsey #19)

Evil Intent (DI Sara Ramsey #20)

The Games People Play (DI Sara Ramsey #21)

I Know The Truth (A Psychological thriller)

She's Gone (A psychological thriller)

Shattered Lives (A psychological thriller)

Evil In Disguise – a novel based on True events

Deadly Act (Hero series novella)

Torn Apart (Hero series #1)

End Result (Hero series #2)

In Plain Sight (Hero Series #3)

Double Jeopardy (Hero Series #4)

Criminal Actions (Hero Series #5)

Regrets Mean Nothing (Hero series #6)

Prowlers (Di Hero Series #7)

Sole Intention (Intention series #1)

Grave Intention (Intention series #2)

Devious Intention (Intention #3)

Cozy mysteries

Murder at the Wedding

Murder at the Hotel

Murder by the Sea

Death on the Coast

Death By Association

Merry Widow (A Lorne Simpkins short story)

It's A Dog's Life (A Lorne Simpkins short story)

A Time To Heal (A Sweet Romance)

A Time For Change (A Sweet Romance)

High Spirits

The Temptation series (Romantic Suspense/New Adult Novellas)

Past Temptation

Lost Temptation

Clever Deception (co-written by Linda S Prather)

Tragic Deception (co-written by Linda S Prather)

Sinful Deception (co-written by Linda S Prather)

ACKNOWLEDGMENTS

Special thanks as always go to @studioenp for their superb cover design expertise.

My heartfelt thanks go to my wonderful editor Emmy, and my proofreaders Joseph and Barbara for spotting all the lingering nits.

Thank you also to my amazing ARC Group who help to keep me sane during this process.

RIP Mum, you've taken a huge part of my heart with you. Until we meet again.

To Mary, gone, but never forgotten. I hope you found the peace you were searching for my dear friend. I miss you each and every day.

PROLOGUE

*S*unday October 22*nd*

THE STUNNING SCENERY all around them made Patricia contemplate the next stage in her life. She hadn't been with her partner, Gertrude, for very long. An all-female partnership was a major turning point in her existence after being married to Mick Wolf for just over twenty years. But Gertrude had opened her eyes to a whole new way of life. Ten years ago, she would have rejected all thoughts of pushing her body to the limits she had this past week. She ached all over, especially her legs, but it was a pain she was willing to push to the side to obtain the 'thrill of the ride' as Gertrude called it.

"Come on, Daydreamer, it's time for us to get on the road. This hill won't conquer itself, get peddling."

"Won't it? I was hoping it might. Crikey, I never dreamt it would be this torturous to climb. Are you sure there isn't a slightly less arduous route we can take?"

"Nope, you're stuck with it. I thought the whole idea of coming away this week was for you to want to feel challenged."

"Did I say that? What the heck was I thinking? The gradient up ahead makes me wonder if I might have lost my mind at the time I agreed to tag along."

Gertrude laughed and muttered something German under her breath. "Life is all about grabbing the challenges ahead of us and overcoming them. We'll feel like failures if we don't."

"So you keep telling me. I thought the hill we encountered yesterday was bad enough, but I've changed my mind since laying eyes on the task facing us. How long do you reckon it's going to take us to get to the top and down the other side?"

"Now you're asking. How long is that piece of string you're always going on about?"

"Okay, point taken. A rough guesstimate would be good for now."

"An hour tops. See, that's all it's going to take to push yourself to your limits."

"I think my aching muscles will tell you that I've achieved that particular ambition already with yesterday's trial. I reckon that was half the size of this one."

Gertrude sighed and shook her head while her foot impatiently flipped the pedal round and round. She looked the part, dressed head to knee in Lycra, fluorescent patches dotted here and there to match her helmet and gloves, ensuring the motorists would see her even on the foggiest of days. "If you want to back out, now is the time to do it, not halfway through the journey. The car is only parked over there. Speak up or get on with it. I'm eager to get on the road."

"Christ, I don't think my life would be worth living if I gave in now, would it?"

Gertrude shrugged, set off and hollered over her shoulder, "Tally ho, and it's off we go. See you on the other side."

"You will... eventually. Don't hang around for me."

"I have no intention of waiting any longer for you. I've set myself a lot of trials this week, I'm not about to start falling by the wayside at this early stage. You told me you wanted to come on this trip to prove something to yourself, right? Well, this is the way to do it. The hills we've tackled this far have been insignificant compared to this one."

"You don't have to drum that into me. I assure you, I can see that with my own two eyes. I'm never one to complain, you know that, but I don't think my muscles will be up for this challenge. I just want to put that out there once and for all."

"We'll see. In this game, there's only one way to attain the unachievable, and that's to put your foot on the pedal and your backside on your saddle and commit to it. I'm off, I'll see you when I see you. I swear you're going to thank me when we get to the top. The views are spectacular, I can tell you. This is one of my favourite hills in the area to travel by bike, a car journey just doesn't do it justice."

"You go. I'll catch up with you. I need five minutes more to psych myself up, if that's all right with you?"

"It is. Think of the reward that lies ahead of you, a superb lunch at The Gather."

Patricia licked her lips. That was all the motivation she needed. They had sampled the delights at the community-run café a few days before. It was considered by locals to be a hidden gem nestled in a stunning location. "I'm there with you, not only in spirit, but I'll also be right behind you."

Gertrude blew her a kiss and winked. "You've got this, my

3

love. Life is about the challenges we seek and overcome." With that, Gertrude began the arduous journey.

Patricia had to conquer her fears and prepare herself for the trial all over again. Two minutes later, and with Gertrude out of sight in front of her, she put her feet on the pedals and set off. The first part of the journey, as expected, took the wind out of her sails. She pulled over in one of the many passing places on the route to have a much-needed drink. There were no views as such, not here. She'd need to motivate herself to get to the middle stage to see the views. The muscles in her legs complained, spasming often as she completed a full rotation of the pedals.

"Why the heck did I agree to this? I'm a mere beginner, and she's an expert cyclist, a vast difference in our abilities, so why the effing hell did I commit to it?" *Because you love her, and when you're in love with someone you often agree to do unthinkable things to appease them.*

Patricia pushed herself and rested again half an hour later, taking in her surroundings now that the low clouds had lifted from their mid-morning start. The views were definitely showing signs of improvement. Even though she was delighted with her achievements so far, the real challenge lay ahead of her, judging by the gradient of the hill facing her on the next leg. The moorland on either side was dotted with grazing sheep, and the odd cow could be made out in the distance.

"There, I'm not alone up here, I have my four-legged friends for company." She laughed and got underway again, thankful there were very few cars around that day, although a number of cyclists had passed her in the last half an hour or so. Recognising she was struggling, they had all shouted words of encouragement at her as they'd whizzed by.

She ploughed on, her legs burning in objection, and dug deep to find the willpower to succeed yet another gruelling leg of her lonely journey. She would have much rather had Gertrude alongside her, cheering her on or kicking her butt; however, she realised the vast difference in proficiency between them and knew it wouldn't be fair to expect Gertrude to lag behind for her benefit.

Patricia finally reached the top of the hill, her heart pounding, another form of objection her body was sending out as a message, punishing her for being daft enough to take on this mammoth task in the first place. One final push, and she knew the amazing views would be worth the crippling effort she'd put in thus far. She was aware that all the hard work was over now; there was a stretch of flat to come, followed by a small hill towards the middle, before the steep descent at the end which would lead her back into the arms of her loved one and a well-earned lunch. The forest to the left was dense, despite the foresters having cleared a few sections here and there. It was blocking the view of Dumfries and Galloway which, she guessed, lay around the next corner.

A sheep decided to cross the road a few feet in front of her. She paused, eager to fill her lungs and let her woolly friend carry on its slow journey. The sound of a car approaching made her cast a glance over her shoulder. She feared for the animal's life and waved her arms, keen for the driver to slow down and appreciate the nature and beauty surrounding them.

So many people are in a hurry these days. If everyone took their foot off life's accelerator now and again to take in the wondrous planet around them, there would be less angst in the world.

The sheep managed to get to the other side of the road unharmed, and Patricia let out a sigh of relief. She scowled at the driver as he flew past her. *Bloody moron... chill, man. What is wrong with people?* Another car popped up in the distance behind her. She decided to remain where she was for the next few minutes to let the driver pass. Her gaze drifted across the nearby moorland, scanning the terrain, watching the sheep grazing and moving on to pastures new.

The car approached her, but instead of going past it slowed down and came to a halt behind her, which wasn't uncommon. There was a patch of ground close by where cars parked up for people to admire the views, or to stop and have a cuppa from a flask, or even to exercise their dogs, but not this individual. The driver revved the engine at her. She studied the area around her, couldn't quite make out what his problem was. The road was double the width at this point, there was no reason at all for him to hound her like this. She turned to look at him and waved him past.

The vehicle inched forward. Patricia decided it was time for her to continue on her journey and pushed off with her right foot. *That should satisfy his impatience. Some people make me sick.*

She soon got up speed going down the hill and rounded the bend, her gaze drawn to the magnificent view. Patricia was enchanted by the scenery that she soon forgot all about the impatient driver. That was until something nudged her rear tyre. She cast a swift glance over her shoulder, and there he was, the driver who had revved his engine at her moments earlier.

She wobbled and shook her fist at him. "What are you doing? Are you bloody insane or what?"

The driver menacingly revved his engine more and then surged forward. Patricia groaned and hit the ground with a thud, her hip landing on a rock sticking out on the side of the road.

"Jesus, you bloody idiot." She rubbed her hip, checking to see if there was any lasting damage. Thankfully, there wasn't.

The driver kept coming, his foot on the accelerator, causing his engine to whine and die intermittently.

"Go past, you bloody shithead. How many times do I have to tell you?"

Patricia's gaze locked on to his. Her gut twisted when she watched his eyes form tiny slits. He sat forward and peered at her whilst gripping the steering wheel. Her heart rate accelerated, the menace she witnessed in his eyes unnerving her. She found herself praying for another cyclist or car to appear to save the day, but the hill remained deserted, except for her and her tormentor.

What the hell am I going to do now? How do I get out of this mess? Gertrude, please come back and save me. Turn around, you must be wondering where I am by now, you must be.

Her thoughts were interrupted by the car inching forward. The driver's revving became far more insistent, so much so that she feared what was about to happen to her.

Crunch! The car's left front tyre crushed the frame of her bike.

"Hey, arsehole! What the fuck is your problem? You're going to pay for that."

The car kept coming. Patricia tried to move back, off the road onto the rough terrain, but her injured hip prevented her. She needed to find a way to battle through the pain and discomfort to get off the road, but how?

The decision was taken out of her hands when the driver put his foot down again, this time catching her ankle. The pain was unbearable. At first, she was too shocked to cry out, to object to what he was doing to her, but it didn't take her long to realise he had no intention of backing off. Her life flashed before her eyes, the twenty-plus years she'd spent with Mark, raising her two teenage children, Lee and Tara, the joy they'd given her until Gertrude had drifted into her life and swept her off her feet.

Where are you, Gertrude? Come and rescue me.

Although she silently pleaded for help, it was obvious it

7

was too late for any hope of rescue. This man had one thing on his mind, to kill her—the evil look in his eyes told her as much.

She decided there was only one option left open to her. Patricia tipped her head back and screamed for help.

CHAPTER 1

"Knock, knock, can I come in?" Bob Jones poked his head into DI Sam Cobb's office.

"Huh, I was miles away. How are things going out there, partner?"

"Sod that. I'm more concerned about you. We've barely seen you this morning. Everything all right, Sam?"

"I'm fine. Deep in thought, and I keep losing myself in my memories. Life sucks. Why can't anything ever be simple? Why does life have a habit of flinging as much shit as it can at you when you least expect it?"

"Pass. Do you want to talk about it? Is it time yet?"

Sam gestured for him to take a seat opposite her. "The simple answer to that is, I'm not sure, Bob. Just when I think I'm ready to deal with my grief, it's as if I'm struck by lightning, and my whole world collapses around me. Does that sound overly dramatic?"

"No, not at all. I'm so sorry, I guess losing a parent is inevitable at our age, but that doesn't mean we're capable of handling it correctly when it happens. How's your dad doing?"

"That's just it, he's been amazing, a real trooper. If I'm honest, I'd have to say that losing Mum hasn't really hit him as such, yet. Maybe organising the funeral and all that entails has kept him occupied, not allowed him to dwell on his loss, who knows? All I keep hearing is that old adage, 'everyone reacts to grief differently'. I suppose that's true if you take on board how my sister and my father are reacting. I'm trying my hardest to steady the ship amidst this torrential monsoon of emotions that are rifling through each and every one of us. Crystal is holding up, but only just. She's really concerned about Dad and the fact that he hasn't sat down with either of us and opened up and cried yet. Men do cry in these instances, don't they? Or is it a case of stiff upper lip and carry on regardless? Life is for living, not brooding over the inevitable when death strikes?"

"Like you say, every family member deals with grief differently, love. I'm sorry you're having to contend with this shit, I truly am. I never had the pleasure of meeting your mum, but if she was anything like you, then I'm sure she was a remarkable and well-loved lady and a force to be reckoned with."

Sam managed a smile for the first time that morning. "I was a tiny kitten compared to my mother. She really had the roar of a lioness. I think that's what I'm going to miss about her the most. Her ability to slap me down whilst still making me feel good about myself, if you get what I mean?"

"I think so. My mum is the same. My sisters and I know when to retreat during an argument, I can tell you. When's the funeral?"

"It still hasn't been decided. There are a few dates flying around, but nothing is set in stone yet. We should hear within the next few days."

"How's Rhys been throughout this?"

"As good as gold. He's definitely stepped up to the plate. I'd be lost without either him, or you, by my side."

Bob coloured up. "Nonsense. I've done nothing."

"Bullshit, you've supported me every day since I broke the news to you. When I realised she was gone, I collapsed into Vernon's arms outside the hospital. He didn't want to be the one to tell me, but I think he loved Mum as much as we did in the end, and he was shellshocked by the events as they had unfolded. We hugged each other and sobbed. I'm grateful for the support he showed all of us on that harrowing day. Had I entered the hospital not knowing… well, I'm not sure how I would have reacted and what effect my reaction might have had on my father and sister. They were staring at the floor when I found them, devastated and utterly bereft. Why does life have to be so damn hard?"

"It certainly tests us at times. I'm so sorry you're going through this Sam, after… losing Chris the way you did."

Sam shook her head. "He doesn't matter, it was his decision to take his own life. There was very little I could have said or done to have persuaded him otherwise. Mum didn't have that option. That drunken bastard, who caused that pile-up in the first place, is the only person to blame for the outcome."

"Hopefully a jury will find him guilty, and he'll rot behind bars. Tossers like that shouldn't be allowed behind the wheel, whether he was cut up about losing his wife and kids or not. Irresponsible bloody jerk. Look how many other lives he destroyed that day, and he walked away from it—well, eventually, after a short spell in hospital with minor cuts and bruises. It's a pity I didn't get to the scene first, before the paramedics. I would have willingly added a few more telling injuries to the list."

"I know. I feel exactly the same as you do. My heart goes

out to the other two families who also lost loved ones that day. I repeat, life can be so unfair at times."

"I understand how galling all of this must be for you, Sam, but there's also that other well-known adage I prefer to live by."

She tilted her head. "Pray tell, oh Wise One."

"Life's too short to sit and wonder. Let's face it, your mother wouldn't want to see you this unhappy, would she?"

His words struck a chord with her; he was absolutely right. Her mother would have been mortified seeing them so distraught with the way they were dealing with her death.

"You're amazing. I don't tell you that nearly enough, partner. You may have a stubborn streak that is hard to overcome most of the time, but every now and again you come out with something so profound, it shocks me to the core."

His cheeks filled with colour once more. "Stop it! You're embarrassing the hell out of me. I'm here for you, Sam. If there's anything I can ever do for you, you only need to give me a yell, and I'll drop anything and everything to help out."

"You're a real friend, Bob. You don't know how much I've valued your kindness over the years and your undeniable friendship."

"I've told you already, you need to stop going all out to embarrass me. I know you're my boss, but I'd like to feel we're more than that... umm... let me rephrase that. That we're friends as well as colleagues."

Sam chuckled. "You can stop digging now. You really struggle with the theory of wearing your heart on your sleeve, don't you?"

"Not sure where you get that ruddy idea from."

They both laughed until Sam suddenly stopped.

"What's up?" he asked, confused.

"I know how silly this is going to sound, but I feel guilty when I'm doing anything but crying."

"Aww... give it time, Sam. I'm sure your mum wouldn't want you to be as miserable as sin. Give yourself a break and a good shake, woman."

"You're a poet and you don't know it." Sam laughed again. "Go, I need to give my head a wobble and get this paperwork sorted ASAP. I've been slacking all morning. Thanks for the pep talk, matey."

"You're welcome. I meant what I said." He patted his right shoulder. "It's always here for you, it's not like I wear expensive suits that you're likely to ruin with your tears."

"You're cracking me up. Thanks, partner. Now go!"

HALFWAY THROUGH THE DAY, at twelve-thirty when her stomach was indicating it must be close to lunchtime, Sam received an unexpected call from a dear friend of hers, Emma Thompson.

"Hey, you, long time no hear. How are tricks over in your beautiful part of the world?"

"Hi, Sam. I'm as busy as ever, but running this place never feels like work. I'm sure you must feel that way some days."

"If you say so. What can I do for you, Emma? It's unusual for you to call me during the day."

"I know. I must admit, I've been pacing the office back and forth all morning, wondering if it was the right thing to ring you or not. You know me, I hate taking advantage of our friendship."

"You never have in the past, so I'm willing to let you off this time round. Come on, spill. What's wrong? You sound anxious about something. If you're seeking advice, I can make an excuse and pop out to see you. It's never a problem; it's been a while since I've had a freebie lunch at your gaff."

"Maybe it would be better to tell you in person. Would you mind?"

"Not at all. Give me thirty minutes, how's that?"

"Perfect. You're the best copper I have the pleasure of knowing. Your expertise will make such a difference to the dilemma."

"Gosh, talking about teasing me. Aren't you going to give me a brief hint?"

"The truth is, I wouldn't know where to start."

"You've definitely piqued my interest now. See you shortly."

"You're a diamond. I don't care what anyone says to the contrary, either."

Sam ended the call and left her chair. She tugged on her jacket, aware of how breezy it could get over at Ennerdale Bridge. Slipping out of the office, she glanced around the room and was pleased to see the rest of the team all with their heads down, hard at work, all except Bob, who was staring straight at her.

She pointed at him. "You, me, lunch at The Gather, on Emma."

"Ooo… now there's an image I'm not likely to dislodge in a hurry," Bob responded, opening his mouth before he'd engaged his brain.

Sam tutted and shook her head. "I'm going to tell Emma you said that when we see her. If you think you're blushing now from that faux pas, it's nothing to what you'll be doing once she finds out."

"Bugger, me and my big mouth. Why do I keep doing that?"

"Let me know when you've figured that out, matey. The rest of you, feel free to grab some lunch when you want, but you know that already, right?"

"Yes, boss. Enjoy your trip out," Claire answered for the rest of the team.

"Oh, we will. Their lunches are phenomenal."

"I remember. Scott and I go over to Ennerdale Water quite a lot, paddleboarding. We've enjoyed many a brunch in there over the years."

"There you go, I learn something new about you all the time, Claire. I've never tried it, I prefer being on dry land to the freezing cold water."

"It has its moments. We don't tend to go down there much when the sun isn't shining."

"You do have some sense then."

They both laughed.

"Umm… I thought we were in a hurry?" Bob said. "My stomach is rumbling here at the thought of having a fresh bacon roll."

Sam tutted and shook her head at the others, walked three paces and gave Bob a friendly nudge in the back to get going. "Come on, I'd hate for you to go hungry. I couldn't stand you complaining all day long."

As PREDICTED, thirty minutes later, Sam drew up in a parking space on the main road leading into the village, rather than take up one of the few places available to the punters directly outside the café. An anxious-looking Emma was there to greet them. Sam and Emma hugged.

"Christ, let me breathe, woman," Sam protested.

"I'm so sorry. I forget my own strength these days. I've been working out in the gym Roger and I had installed a few years ago. It's great to see you again, Sam, it's been far too long. I hope you didn't mind me ringing you. I was at a loss who to turn to, we all are."

Sam backed away from her old school chum. "The more you say about the situation, the more intrigued I become. Why don't you tell me what's going on over a cuppa, Emma?"

"And throw in a bacon roll or two," Bob muttered as a hint beside her.

"Of course. Come in." Emma placed the order at the counter, and one of the regular members of staff, Helen, got to work in the small kitchen area, belting out a song.

It had always amazed Sam how they managed to churn out the vast number of orders they received each day in such a diddy, confined space. Emma led them to the back of the café which was half empty. The three of them pulled out a chair at the table set out for six visitors.

"What's all this about, Emma? I don't think I've ever seen you look this worried in your life before."

"In all honesty, it has knocked me for six." Emma leaned forward and lowered her voice. "Yesterday, one of the cyclists exploring the area came in for lunch. I noticed while I was serving the other customers, she was keeping a watchful eye on the door and was constantly glancing at her watch. You know me, ever the inquisitive sort, I cleared and wiped down the table next to her and tried to strike up a conversation with her. She was super distracted, didn't even hear me talking to her at first, not until I moved position and stood in her line of sight. She dodged sideways to fix her gaze on the entrance again."

Emma shuddered and then continued. "I could tell there was something seriously wrong; I couldn't leave it there. So, I took the liberty of sitting in the chair opposite her and gently asked if there was anything wrong. Her eyes immediately filled up with tears, and she broke her gaze momentarily to stare down at her cup of coffee, which by then had unfortunately gone cold. I called over to Helen to get the lady a top-up. She smiled at me and said, 'It's my partner, I'm concerned about her. We set off from Calderbridge over three hours ago, and she hasn't arrived yet.' Well, that was yesterday lunchtime. I told her that I would organise a search party

16

amongst the locals. They did me proud, turned out in force, looked everywhere, on foot, quad bikes, Range Rovers, bikes, the lot, and no, there was no sign of either Patricia or the bike she was riding. In the end, at around seven last night, I told Gertrude she needed to call the police. Which she did, only to be told to ring back today. She was told an officer would go to check but hasn't heard anything since."

"Where's Gertrude now?" Sam asked. She glanced around the occupied tables to see if there was anyone dining alone.

"She's staying at the Fox and Hounds. I told her that I would get in touch with you and see if there was anything further we could do about her partner, Patricia's, disappearance. Gertrude told me she hasn't slept all night. She's been ringing Patricia's phone constantly throughout the night, and nothing. The phone eventually died at eight this morning, heightening Gertrude's concern for her partner. I rang her after I spoke to you, informed her that you were on your way over here, and she's nipped back to the hotel to freshen up. She'll be back in twenty minutes or so."

"Enough time for us to shove a bacon roll down our necks," Bob said in his ever-persistent manner.

Sam groaned and found herself apologising for her partner's behaviour. "He can't think straight when he's running on empty."

Emma cracked a smile. "Typical man, right. Your lunch won't be long, Bob. The service is always prompt around here."

Bob rubbed his stomach and plucked some sugar sachets from the jar in the middle of the table ready for when his drink showed up.

"Poor woman. Mind you, it's not the easiest journey to make, cycling Cold Fell, and I take it there's been no sightings of her since?"

"A couple of the locals, the odd ones who cycle the route

regularly, said they believe they passed her and shouted words of encouragement because she appeared to be struggling, and another of the locals, Jim, said he passed her up near the forest. She was taking a break and sipping from her water bottle."

"I'll need to speak with anyone who saw her. Are they around, or am I pushing my luck there?"

"Jim's been in this morning, really concerned about her, told me he was intending to go out there again to have another scout around. He's brilliant, really knows the area like the back of his hand, having lived in the village most of his life."

"Always handy having a local willing to do all they can for a total stranger," Bob chipped in.

"He's not the only one who was out there. At least thirty of the villagers went out over the course of the afternoon and evening, and they all returned with the same response: Patricia was nowhere to be seen."

Their coffees arrived, and Emma smiled and thanked the younger waitress.

Bob glanced over his shoulder in the direction of the kitchen, and Sam covered a hand over his, making him jump.

"Jesus, don't do that, you scared the doodah out of me."

"Do da?" Sam queried with a smile. "Do brave coppers say that?"

"This one does. It's what we used to say when Milly was younger, it's kind of stuck."

Helen came out of the kitchen area with a plate in each hand and veered off to the right of their table at the last minute. "Here you go, fill your boots."

"Damn, I thought our luck was in then. I bet this Gertrude shows up before we've had a chance to sink our teeth into our rolls."

As if he'd tempted fate, Emma pointed at the door. "Here she is now. Hi, Gertrude, over here."

The tall, slender woman headed their way at a brisk pace and slotted into the chair beside Emma.

"Gertrude, I'd like to introduce DI Sam Cobbs, an old school friend of mine, and her partner, Bob."

"Not so much of the old," Sam said. She reached out a hand for Gertrude to shake. "Pleased to meet you. We're here to assist you in any way we can."

Gertrude released the breath she appeared to be sucking in. "I can't thank you all enough for taking me seriously. There's no reason for Patricia to go missing like this. We're here on a cycling holiday. She is up for the challenge, although she's not as experienced as I am. She urged me to go on ahead yesterday and insisted that she would catch up with me here, to have lunch. I feel so bad for forcing her to do this ride. The longer the delay, the more anxious I became. Emma has been an absolute star, organising a search party. Everyone has been so kind and thoughtful. I'm a nobody to them, but that hasn't stopped them going out of their way to assist me."

"I'm detecting an accent there, Gertrude, are you German?"

"That's right. I've lived and worked in the UK for over twenty years, so I consider myself a Brit through and through these days."

"And what about Patricia? Is she German as well? Not that it matters, of course."

"No, she's English. We've only been together for the past six months."

"And you say you're on holiday in the area?"

"Yes. This was a special treat that Patricia arranged for my birthday which is coming up next weekend, only we couldn't

19

make it then as I have a meeting in London I need to attend. I'm a consultant, and we live in Manchester."

"Ah, I see."

The waitress brought their bacon rolls, and Bob groaned, aware that his was likely to go cold.

"Please, eat your lunch. I need to make a phone call or two. I'll join you again in a moment. Enjoy, they're the best bacon rolls in the area, I can vouch for that." Gertrude smiled and rose from her seat before Sam got the chance to try and persuade her to stick around.

"Thank you. We won't be long," Sam said.

Emma stood and winked at Sam. "I've got a bit of paperwork to catch up on in the office. We'll both be back soon."

Emma accompanied Gertrude to the exit where they had a brief chat and then went their separate ways.

Bob took a bite out of his roll. A blob of ketchup escaped the side and slid down his chin. He reached for his serviette and had the decency to mop up the mess swiftly, without her needing to plead with him. "What do you make of her?" he said between bites.

"She seems decent enough. Concerned for her partner's well-being, as any person would be. Why? What are you picking up from the briefest of interviews with her?"

"All right, there's no need to say it like that. I only asked the question."

"What is it that's rankling you, the fact she's a lesbian or is it because she's German?"

Bob's mouth gaped open, and Sam turned her head away.

"Do you mind? How much have you bloody shoved in there?"

"Damn, one criticism after another today. If that's the thanks I get for showing any kind of concern for you earlier, remind me not to bother in the future."

"Sorry, that was uncalled for. Come on, speaking openly. What's your problem, if you have one?"

"I don't, all I asked was a simple question, and you jumped all over me."

"Sorry, fair point. Maybe I misread your question."

"It's the same question I always ask once we've interviewed someone relating to a crime... correction, who has reported a crime, if that's what this is." He took another chunk out of his roll.

Sam had barely touched hers. Her appetite seemed to have waned slightly since speaking with Gertrude. "It does seem strange that she left Patricia behind while she set off up over the moorland alone, not something I would dream of doing to a partner with less experience who might need to reach out for a helping hand along the way, but each to their own, eh?"

"My thoughts exactly. Why would you do that? What's the point in going on a cycling holiday as a couple, if all you're going to do is up and leave the more inexperienced partner to handle a tricky terrain like Cold Fell?"

Sam munched on her bacon roll, lost in thought. *Maybe there's more to Patricia's disappearance than meets the eye. Only together six months... very suspicious.*

"What are you thinking?" Bob asked conspiratorially.

Sam winked. "Never you mind. Let's not make any rash judgements at this stage of the game. We'll see how the rest of the day turns out first. How's your lunch?"

"Bloody lovely, although I have to say, a second one wouldn't go amiss."

Sam pulled away pieces of her own roll, around where her lips had touched, and then shoved the rest of it towards Bob. "Have mine, I appear to have lost my appetite."

Her partner didn't need telling twice and ripped into the bun as if he'd just been rescued from a desert island, where

21

food had been sparse for months on end. "Thanks, this will fill a hole, for a while at least."

"You pig. How can you eat like that in public?"

"Easy, I'll show you."

Sam had seen, and heard, enough. She left the table, taking her cup and saucer with her, and knocked on the office door at the other end of the café to have a chat with Emma.

"Come in."

Sam eased open the door and poked her head into the cramped office. "Room for a little one?"

Emma laughed. "Barely. Squeeze in, if you can. You haven't eaten your lunch already, have you?"

"Half of it, the rest I contributed to my partner and his far-from-full stomach."

"You used to be the same at school. Once the boys gave you a puppy-dog-eye look, you instantly handed over your packed lunch."

Sam shrugged. "Guilty as charged. Back in the day, I was always a sucker for a good sob story."

Emma reached out a hand. "You were. It used to drive me to distraction. Your heart has always been too good for those around you. Enough about our long-distant past, what's new with you, anything? We haven't been in touch for a while. How's Chris?"

Sam chewed on her lip and, Emma being Emma, cottoned on quickly that there was something wrong.

"No, aren't you guys together any more?"

"Umm... correct. Chris died."

Emma sprang forward in her comfy office chair. "What? How? Why didn't you ring me? I would have been there for you, Sam. God, I feel terrible now. Sorry if I've opened some old wounds."

Sam was shocked to find tears flowing down her

cheeks. Emma took her in her arms and hugged her, much harder than she had when Sam and Bob had arrived. It took a while for Sam to compose herself enough to push away.

"I'm sorry. I feel I must explain myself. These tears aren't for Chris, they're for my mother. She died a couple of weeks ago in a car crash, along with two other people."

"Bloody hell. What the heck? Poor you. My heart goes out to you. I wish you'd called me, I would have offered you all the support you needed to tackle your mother's death after losing Chris. Dare I ask how he died? You don't have to tell me if you'd rather not."

"It's fine. He committed suicide." Sam held a hand up as Emma's mouth opened once more. "You need to hear all the facts before you show that bastard any sympathy, love."

"And they are?"

"He did the dirty on me. Ended up shacked up with another woman, a solicitor, he had previously done some work for. She soon got bored of him and kicked him out. I had moved on by then, and he couldn't hack me being with someone else. You know how it is, he didn't want me but didn't want anyone else having me either. He showed up at the cottage we bought together, pleaded with me to take him back, and when I refused, he bloody poured petrol over himself and lit a match."

"Good grief. What a mixed-up individual he must have been towards the end of his life."

"His fault entirely. I refuse to feel guilty about the way he decided to go out. What was equally upsetting at the time, was that Rhys had not long drawn up and parked beside him. My fella got out of the car to make sure I was okay, and boom! Both cars exploded... inside Rhys's car was his beloved dog."

"It gets bloody worse. I feel so bad for you, having to

contend with all that shit. Why didn't you tell any of the old gang? We would have been there for you at a drop of a hat."

"I know you would have. I just needed to deal with the debacle myself. After Rhys lost his dog in the explosion, he couldn't handle having a relationship with me and walked out of my life. I was left feeling bereft and lost in the wilderness because I'd fallen heavily for him over the few months we were together."

"Oh, Sam. My heart is breaking for you. This all sounds like a macabre Mills and Boon story."

"But... who should show up at Chris's funeral, asking to be forgiven? Only Rhys. Needless to say, Chris's parents weren't too happy when we embraced after the service."

"Sod them. You have a right to grasp happiness while you're still young enough to enjoy it. Umm... did I really say that? I think I channelled my mum with that quote."

They both laughed.

Sam removed a tissue from her jacket pocket and wiped the tears that had settled on her cheeks. "God, I've missed you so much. I'm kicking myself for losing touch with you. We swore when we were in our teens, we'd never allow that to happen, didn't we?"

"I remember that day well. We were a tad inebriated as I recall."

"Ah, yes, that part conveniently slipped my mind. Enough about us, tell me what your instinct is about what's gone on with Gertrude and this partner of hers."

"What do you mean? Are you saying that something seems out of place to you?"

"Far too early to tell. I suppose I'm guilty of erring on the side of caution. How many cyclists do you know, who would have the nerve to go missing when there's a lunch at The Gather on offer?"

Emma tipped her head back and laughed. "You're an idiot.

You had me worried then. I consider myself a good judge of character and I wondered if my radar had gone haywire for a moment or two. We're talking what? An eight-mile stretch by road. Okay, the terrain is rough in places, there's a huge forest to consider and vast moorland that goes on for miles as well… heck, I've just talked myself out of my reasoning, so ignore me."

"Shall we call the area unforgiving? We're going to put the fabulous views from the top aside for a while."

"I'd say unforgiving is perfect, especially on a cold, foggy day or when the hills are draped in low clouds; it can be quite foreboding up there."

Sam gave an involuntary shudder. "Don't, I can imagine. I've only ever travelled the route on a bright summer's day. Right, I'd better see if Gertrude is up to speaking to us yet, or more to the point if Bob has demolished his, and my, lunch yet."

"He seems a good man," Emma said.

"He has his moments. He's been wonderful with me lately, during the grieving process."

"I'm glad to hear it. Don't forget, I'm only at the end of the phone, if you need me. Isn't that what friends are supposed to be for?"

"I know. Consider me told. I didn't feel as though I should burden anyone, other than family and perhaps the odd work colleague, with my grief."

"Friends, and this friend in particular, should have been high up on that list of yours. It's not too late. Give me a call this evening. Roger is going out tonight, so I'll be on my lonesome."

"Thanks, Emma. I'll see what goes on with the rest of my day first. That's the trouble with policing, you can't make any immediate plans if something like this rears its head."

"I can imagine. The offer is still on the table all the same."

They hugged a final time.

"You're a true friend, thanks."

Sam left the office, and her gaze was immediately drawn to Bob looking her way. Opposite him, Gertrude had returned to the table. Sam suppressed the giggle threatening to emerge, aware of how uncomfortable her partner must be feeling with an emotional woman to entertain in her absence. She made her way through the café to rescue him.

As suspected, Gertrude appeared to be down and possibly reminiscent.

"I'm back. How are you, Gertrude?"

Gertrude forced out a smile. "Confused, distraught. I have to say I'm going through a whole gamut of emotions at this time. Is that normal?"

"Unfortunately, yes. Until you're reunited with your partner, I predict your emotions and thoughts are going to be all over the place. Where were you staying?"

"At the Fox and Hounds, nothing has changed there. When I go back to our room, I'm surrounded by her stuff which is a constant reminder that she's missing. I much prefer hanging out around here, and Emma and the staff have been brilliant. I wouldn't say that I'm pestering the customers but I'm discreetly enquiring if any of the cyclists have possibly sighted Patricia en route over the fell." Her head dipped, and her chin touched her chest. "I can't believe she'd go off and leave me stranded here. That doesn't make any sense. She was thrilled to be here. Okay, she complained before we set off that she was a little achy; maybe I should have listened to her complaint rather than dismissing it. Perhaps if I had done that we'd be sitting here together now." Her head lifted, and she swallowed. "I miss her so much. I know we haven't been together long, but she has quickly become my soulmate. Maybe that's why this has hit me so hard."

Sam covered Gertrude's shaking hand with her own. "I know it's probably not what you want to hear right now, but try not to get too upset. It's imperative that you remain positive. It's going to be a very bumpy road ahead of you if you don't."

"I appreciate what you're saying. I'll do my very best to try and keep my emotions in check. I'm going to have to, they're due soon."

Sam frowned. "Who are?"

"Patricia's family. I was torn as to whether I should inform them now or wait for further news. I decided it would be better to be upfront with them from the outset. Her husband—yes, they're still married—Mick is travelling up from Manchester with their two teenage children, Lee and Tara."

"Do you get on well with them?"

Gertrude worried her lip with her front teeth and shook her head. "Not the husband for obvious reasons. I swooped in and stole her while he was sleeping, I think that's how I would put it. His emotions were tuned out from the relationship, that's how Patricia explained it. They hadn't been intimate with each other in years."

"I see. Can I ask how you met?"

"We worked on separate floors in the same building and got talking in the lift one day. I'm a management consultant, and she's an IT manager. I had a problem with a software package I was using in the office. She said she'd come up and have a look at it for me at the end of the day. We hit it off right away, and I bought her a drink at the wine bar across the road from the office to say thank you for getting me out of a jam, the rest is history. We clicked; neither of us had ever been with a woman before. I divorced my husband nearly five years ago because something didn't feel right. I had no idea I would feel the way I do about another woman, but I suppose we can never tell who we're going to fall in love with, can we?"

"What about the children?"

"The children are very hip, they've accepted me as their mother's new and permanent partner, the total opposite to Mick. He blames me, of course he does, I swept his wife off her feet. But I still maintain that if Patricia had still been in love with Mick and, more to the point, if Mick had shown her more attention, then she wouldn't have been tempted in the first place."

Sam nodded, understanding completely the draw of having someone new who showed an interest in you. The same thing had happened to her when she had met Rhys at the local park where they had shared their first kiss while she was still married to Chris. She shook her head to dislodge the memory. "I agree, there are times when we can no longer deny what the heart desires."

"It sounds like you're speaking from experience, Inspector?" Gertrude said, her head tilting to the side.

Sam smiled. "Maybe. Going back to her family, when are they due to arrive?"

Gertrude checked her texts on her mobile. "Lee messaged me about an hour ago, said they were just coming off the motorway, so I think they will be here soon, at least within the next twenty minutes or thereabouts. I'm not sure if I did the right thing calling them or not. I found myself in a true dilemma, but I wouldn't have been able to forgive myself if I hadn't got in touch, at least with the kids. That's who I reached out to in the first place. I texted Lee, and he said it wouldn't be right to keep the news from his father. It took me a while to see his point of view and to agree that it was the right way forward. I never dreamt they would get on the road and come up here. I hope Mick doesn't cause any trouble. I'm going through enough stress as it is without having to deal with the amount he's likely to add to my load. If that's the right term. Sometimes the proper English term escapes me, especially when I'm stressed."

"Hey, I'd say you've coped pretty well up until now. Hang in there. When they arrive, I can take Mick aside and have an official word with him, if you think that will help?"

Gertrude's gaze drifted out of the window to the spectacular view, and she sighed. "I think that might do just the opposite, but what do I know? I've never been in such a difficult situation as this before."

"It's hard to judge, granted. We all deal with our emotions differently. Maybe the kids will help out and try and keep their father calm."

Gertrude turned her attention to Sam once more and nodded. "I think they'll do their best to step in, if and when it's needed. They've been amazing with me, included me in everything when they've visited their mother."

"Do you have a place together?"

"Yes, Patricia moved all her clothes into my tiny apartment in Manchester. We're in the process of searching for a bigger one, but it's a mammoth task in the city. We're considering going further afield, buying a property of our own on the outskirts of Manchester. I'd love to go more rural, but Patricia isn't too keen on that idea. She's a city girl, whereas I was brought up in the country in Germany. My parents owned a small farm. I presume that's why places like this pull at my heartstrings and I have an urgency running through me to explore these types of surroundings. I suppose you'd say it was in my blood. I loathe living in the city but consider it as a necessary evil. I'm trying to organise my workload so that I can work from home more. At the moment, I do three days in the office and two at home." Something caught her eye, and she shuffled uncomfortably in her seat. "They're here."

Sam followed Gertrude's gaze and spotted a man heading towards them at full speed.

"Any news?" he demanded.

"Dad, at least say hello first. Hi, Gertrude," a young man said.

He gripped his father's forearm, but his father shrugged him off.

"Whatever. Any news on my wife? Is she still missing?"

"Hello, Mick, yes, Patricia is still missing," Gertrude said, her voice shaking. "This is Detective Inspector Cobbs and her partner. They've come to help us."

"Oh, have they now? And pray tell me why the bloody hell you're all sitting on your arses in here rather than being out there, searching for her."

Sam didn't feel the need to extend her hand for him to shake, fearing it might be rejected. "Why don't you take a seat? Can we get you a drink after your long journey?"

"No. I demand to know what's going on. Why you're all in here and not out there," he repeated. "What, are you hoping she'll still find her way here, after all this time? Jesus, what are we dealing with here? Keystone Cops who haven't got a clue, or what?"

Sam nudged Bob with her knee under the table. She could tell how irate he was becoming beside her. "There's no need for that kind of talk, sir. We arrived not long ago and were just running through the events of what happened with Gertrude."

"She's to blame. None of this would have happened and my wife would still be with us, *as a family*, if she hadn't flashed her eyes and other parts of her anatomy at Patricia in the first place."

Sam sighed inwardly. "The rights and wrongs of what has gone on in the past isn't what matters here, sir. Patricia's well-being and finding her should be our only consideration now."

"Which is why I asked why you're all sitting around, doing fuck all to find her." Mick inched forward.

Bob jumped to his feet and pointed. "You're going to need to take a step back and calm down, sir. And I'd also advise you to treat these ladies with the respect they deserve."

Mick glared at Bob but didn't back down.

"Let's not blow this out of all proportion," Sam interjected. "Take a seat, and we'll discuss the matter calmly. If you're unable to do that, sir, I'm going to have to ask you to leave."

"You can't do that. I have a right to know where my wife is."

"I'm afraid you don't. You and your wife are separated. She's moved on with her life and found a new love who she appears to be content with."

"You've only got her word for that." Mick jabbed a finger in Gertrude's direction.

"And that's good enough for me," Sam bit back.

The young lady standing behind her father started crying. "Dad, I don't want all of this. Why did we bother coming all this way if not to help out? I just want to find Mum and get back home to Manchester."

Mick closed his eyes for the briefest of moments and then lowered himself into the chair furthest away from Gertrude. His two children sighed and filled the other two seats.

"I'm not going to apologise for my actions. We're all distraught about Patricia going missing."

"I couldn't have put it better myself," Gertrude agreed. "We want the same thing at the end of the day—Patricia's safe return."

Mick nodded his agreement, and his shoulders slouched,

intimating to Sam that he was finally admitting that he might be guilty of overreacting.

"Where do we go from here?" Mick asked, his tone far from normal, but nevertheless, much improved.

"There are several witnesses we need to speak with. Once we've interviewed everyone then we'll have a clearer picture of what's going on."

"Where are these witnesses?"

"Around. It shouldn't take us too long. In the meantime, I'm going to need you to be patient with us."

Mick jumped to his feet, tipping his chair over in the process. Every customer surrounding them turned to look their way.

"I refuse to hang around here doing sod all. Come on, kids."

"But, Dad, I'm hungry and thirsty. We've had a long trip up here," Lee whined.

Mick righted his chair, flopped into it and crossed his arms. "All right, you win, this time. You've got twenty minutes, and then I'm off."

Lee held his hand out. "I need some money."

"Nothing new there, then," his father sneered at him. He pulled a twenty from his wallet and threw it on the table. "I'll have a flat white coffee; I couldn't stomach anything to eat."

"What do you want, Tara?" Lee asked his sister.

"If they have a tuna sandwich, I'll have one of those on brown and a Coke, please."

Lee went up to the counter and ordered, leaving behind him a frosty atmosphere at the table.

Sam felt obliged to strike up a conversation with Mick. "Did the journey take you long?"

"Long enough. Holdups on the M6."

Sam smiled. "As usual. I want to personally thank you and your son and daughter for being here. I'm sure Patricia will appreciate her nearest and dearest being around when we finally find her."

"Don't you mean *if* she's found?" Mick retorted swiftly.

Gertrude shuffled in her seat opposite Sam, clearly biting her tongue.

"We're going to do our utmost to bring her back to you."

Mick cocked an eyebrow and mumbled, "Yeah, it looks like it."

Sam felt relieved when she saw Emma walking towards her with a tall, thin man.

"Sam, I'd like to introduce you to Jim, he's one of the main witnesses I was telling you about."

Sam leapt out of her seat and shook the man's hand. He grinned, showing off a single top tooth.

"Pleased to meet you, Jim. Umm... I should have asked earlier, Emma, is there somewhere we can use to interview the witnesses?"

"My office is too small. I can open up the Community Room upstairs, would that do?"

"That would be great. Thanks."

"Follow me, I'll nip and get the key. Two ticks."

Bob and Sam left the table.

"Hey, what about us?" Mick shouted.

"We shouldn't be too long. Enjoy your lunch in the meantime."

"He's going to be trouble," Bob whispered in her ear.

"Grin and bear it, partner. We've overcome his sort before."

"I could hang around out here and give him a good slap if you want me to."

Sam laughed. "I can see that going down well with his family and the locals."

CHAPTER 2

*E*mma exited her office and dangled the key in front of her. "Come with me. Are you all right with the stairs, Jim?"

"Exactly how old do you think I am, Emma?"

Emma sniggered. "Sorry, me and my big mouth."

Emma unlocked the door at the top of the stairs and switched on the lights. "I hope this will suffice. We use it quite often for gatherings and local meetings, plus the odd exhibition now and again. The place is free for the next week or so, just in case you need to use it longer than today."

"Worth knowing," Sam said. "This will do great, Emma, thanks."

Emma left them to it.

"Why don't we take a seat, Jim?"

The three of them sat around one of the available square tables. Bob removed his notebook from his pocket and flipped it open.

"Jim, I'm DI Sam Cobbs, and this is my partner, Bob Jones. Thank you for taking the time to come here today to help us with our enquiries."

"Not a problem. I've been out there this morning, poor woman."

"Emma said you passed Patricia up on Cold Fell, is that correct?"

"Yes, she appeared to be struggling. I'd say she looked more knackered than just tired. I offered to give her a lift, but she turned me down, told me that she hadn't got all the way to the top just to give in. She was going to have a breather and a drink before ploughing on. I have to admit, the hard part was over for her. I still thought I'd show willing, though."

"That was kind of you. Can you tell me exactly where this was?"

"On the rough patch of ground, the pull-in at the top, right by the forest."

"I know the part," Bob said.

"Were there any other vehicles around there at the time?"

"No, it's usually quiet up there on a Sunday morning. Most likely all the folks were otherwise engaged, visiting morning mass." He laughed. "I'm joking, not sure many folks go to church these days, not round here."

"Not like the old days, eh?" Sam agreed.

"That's right. However, most people find time for exercise, either cycling or fell-walking around these parts nowadays."

"Emma mentioned that you've lived here most of your life. I bet you've seen a few changes over the years."

"I have, and I've had the pleasure of talking with thousands of tourists visiting the area. We thrive on having people coming here. It's not too crowded in the summer, not like other parts of The Lakes, you know, further north or over to the east. It's good for the businesses in this area if the tourists keep coming. But that won't be the case if this woman isn't found. What do you suppose happened to her?

35

There was no need for her to go missing, to veer off the road, not unless she stopped for a private moment; perhaps she drank too much and nature called. Not nice when you're caught short like that, is it? I suggested the same to Emma. She thought I was joking, but I was deadly serious. It's much easier for men to go to the loo out in the open than it is for women."

Sam smiled. "It's not something that's ever crossed my mind. I used to do a lot of fell-walking a few years ago and I always made sure I took a camping urinal with me. Don't ask."

Bob chuckled but didn't call her on it.

"Where there's a will," Jim replied. "Not a contraption I'd fancy using if ever I considered going camping."

"You said you've been out there this morning, for long?"

"An hour or so. I concentrated on the higher area because that's where I saw her last. Searched along the road, behind the stone walls, hoping I'd find her bike, but nothing. It's as if she vanished into thin air."

"Have you heard of this sort of thing happening in the past?"

His mouth drooped at the sides, then he shook his head after a moment or two of thinking time. "Never... No, that's not quite true. I seem to recall a bunch of kids going missing while they were on a camping trip up there. They got separated from their classmates. It turned out to be for only a few hours and all was good in the end. Scared the crap out of the youngsters, I believe."

"I bet it did. Was that down to the weather conditions at the time?"

He frowned, contemplating her question. "I think it was. Yes, it was a dreary November day, and the fog had rolled in from the sea. Again, a bunch of us locals went up there to help with the search and rescue. It was old Sid who found them, God rest his soul. He passed away a few months after that through bowel cancer. Vile bloody disease."

"That's a shame. The locals, you included, appear to be a caring bunch."

A glimmer of a smile touched his lips. "We do our best. None of us are experts, and thankfully we're not called into action that often, but when we are, we drop everything and get up there."

"You're to be admired. I'm not sure every village throughout the UK would have such a caring community as you have here, especially not these days. Everyone seems to lead a hectic life and has little time on their hands to spend hours searching for a total stranger."

"I've never really stopped to think about it. I've been a farmer for years, and yes, we have some spare time on our hands between dealing with our livestock, but we're just as busy as other folks at the end of the day."

"I bet more so, during important periods of the year. Are you retired now?"

"Yes, I sold my flock a couple of years ago. I've still got my farm. I think I'm going to sell up soon. With little to no income, I'm struggling to meet the bills as they've skyrocketed lately. Damn cost-of-living crisis."

Sam sighed. "It's hit everyone hard, in all walks of life."

"If you say so. I don't think trade has dropped off around here at this place, but what do I know? Emma and her team take care of their customers well, always have done. The locals use this place as much as the tourists."

"So I've heard. Is your farm very far?"

"A couple of miles out of the village at the top of the hill." He thumbed behind him.

"Is there anything else you can tell us about Patricia and your sighting of her yesterday?"

"Not really, I think I've told you everything."

"Okay, then again I want to thank you for coming to see us today and for all the effort you've put in to search for Patricia, it truly is appreciated."

"Anyone with an ounce of compassion for people would do the same, there's really no need for anyone to thank me. I have time on my hands, so what else am I going to do?"

Sam smiled. "Enjoy the rest of your day."

"I'll go home and have a rest for an hour or so and then get back out there for another scout around, providing she hasn't been found by then. Will you guys be sorting out a search of your own?"

"Yes, we'll get that organised ASAP."

"Good. She needs to be found. Maybe she had a fall and is suffering from amnesia and just wandering the moorland up there."

"That's definitely a possibility we should consider, going forward." Sam stood and extended her hand. "Thanks again, Jim."

The three of them left the room and walked back down the stairs. Jim set off for home and jumped into his black SUV.

"Give me a second to check in with Emma," Sam said. "Can you ring the station and organise a search party, Bob?"

"Leave it with me." He drifted around the back of the building, to the small seating area overlooking the open fields, to make his call.

Sam entered the café and knocked on the office door.

"Come in," Emma bellowed.

"It's only me. All done with old Jim, he seemed a nice man. Any idea where I can find the other witnesses?"

Emma winked. "I took the liberty of giving them a call, and they're inside having a coffee. I'll come and introduce you to them. I think they're eager to get on their way."

"Great. I won't hold them up too long."

After Emma had introduced Sam to the other witnesses, she took them upstairs to the room Emma had provided and questioned them individually.

Dave Thomas was the first to be interviewed.

"You saw the missing lady, Patricia, yesterday?"

"Yes, I passed her. I was on my bike, going a lot faster, and shouted words of encouragement. I feel guilty for not stopping to check if she was all right now, after what's happened."

"Please don't, it's not your fault she's gone missing. Did she speak to you?"

"She waved and shouted thanks in response, and I went on ahead. I know you say I shouldn't feel guilty, but that's easier said than done. If anything untoward has happened to her up there, it's going to haunt me for the rest of my life."

"I feel the same way," the other man said, obviously listening in to their conversation.

"You shouldn't, these things happen from time to time. We're remaining positive that we will find her. Are you a cyclist, too, Matt?" Sam called across the room.

"Yes, although we weren't together up there. I've become friends with Dave since all this occurred. We went up there yesterday before it got dark. It was hopeless, we couldn't see her, no sign of her bike either. It's flummoxed me how someone can just disappear like that."

"Hopefully, we'll get to the bottom of that soon." She glanced up to see Bob enter the room. Sam turned her attention back to Dave. "Where are you from?"

"Blackpool. I quite often venture over this way at various times of the year."

"And you're travelling alone?"

"That's right. My wife was unable to join me on this trip, although she frequently tags along. She's an experienced cyclist, too. I don't think the lady in question seemed very confident in charge of the bike. In my opinion, she should have had a companion with her. That hill is steeper than most people think when they attempt to conquer it. I'd say it's one of the most challenging in the area."

"I'd agree to that, in certain parts," Matt said.

"And where are you from, Matt?"

"Birmingham area, just on the outskirts really, although I work in the city itself. I come up to The Lakes a couple of times a year. This is the first time I've stayed around here and tackled the hills, though."

"Are you alone on this trip?"

"No, my girlfriend is with me. She prefers wandering around the shops to putting her body through extreme pressure." He laughed.

Sam joined in. "I know the type. I used to do a lot of fell-walking myself. Always got saddle sore riding a bike so tend to steer clear of it these days, having learnt my lesson the hard way. I won't go into gory details, but it wasn't pleasant."

"That's when you need an expert's advice. Any cycle shop with a good reputation would have assisted you, ensured you had a suitable saddle for your rear, so to speak."

"Had I known that was a thing I would have sought out advice. Anyway, when you both passed Patricia, did either of you notice anyone else hanging around close to her?"

"Plenty of sheep, but no humans," Dave replied. "I should have helped her in some way. I figured if she took her time she'd get to her destination eventually. Imagine my horror when I heard the news that she'd gone missing."

"Yeah, it was a tough call to make for both of us," Matt added. "You never think you'll hear about someone going missing, not in a beautiful place like this, and especially not on a reasonably clear day."

"Thankfully, it isn't a regular occurrence, but when it does happen it makes everyone stop and think. That's when the what-ifs are bandied around. Is there anything else you can tell us?"

Both men shook their heads.

"I can't speak for Matt, but my encounter with her was a brief one, around fifteen seconds, no more than that."

Matt nodded in agreement. "Mine, too. Maybe I should have hung around a bit longer to make sure she progressed further under her own steam. She told me she was fine and enjoying the scenery, so I left her to it."

"Had she made it up to the forest by then?" Sam asked.

"No, I'd say she was about ten minutes from reaching that point."

"That's helpful to know, thanks. Okay, we don't want to hold you gents up any longer than is necessary. I can't thank you enough for sticking around to speak with us."

"It's okay, glad to have been of some assistance," Dave replied.

"That goes for me, too," Matt said.

The four of them descended the stairs once more, and Sam shook the gents' hands at the bottom and wished them a pleasant journey home.

"I get the feeling we're not going to get very far until the real search gets underway," Bob said.

"I've got my doubts if that's going to make a difference or not. Let's face it, if the locals couldn't find her, what hope have our lot got? All strangers to the area."

Bob heaved out a breath. "It's a bloody mystery, that's what it is. People don't go missing like she has, not when they appear to be happy."

"I hear you. Unless..." Sam glanced over her shoulder to check there was no one within earshot of what she was about to say next.

"Go on," Bob asked impatiently.

"Unless she fell out with Gertrude before they set off."

"And that's why she went ahead of her? Sounds plausible. Of course, there's the other scenario that we need to consider as well."

"Which is?"

Bob leaned in and whispered, "That the husband did it."

Sam screwed up her nose and shook her head. "But he was back in Manchester."

Bob shrugged. "It's about a three-hour drive, doable in a day to drive all this way and get back home before someone notices you're missing. Might be worth asking what his itinerary consisted of yesterday."

"Christ, you're right. I bet we're going to take some stick for it, though. He seems the type to fly off the handle at the drop of a hat."

"Maybe that's just with Gertrude. His ego has been injured. I think I'd feel the same way if Abigail went off with another woman, and you'd probably react the same way if Rhys went off with another fella, and don't try and deny it."

Sam held her hands up in front of her. "I wouldn't dream of it. I suppose it's safe to say none of us know how we would react to a situation like that, it's not something I've ever considered. It was bad enough when I found out Chris was cheating on me with another woman, but that's a different matter entirely. Christ, forget I even brought that up."

Bob smiled. "It's forgotten. You get where I'm coming from, though, don't you?"

"Yes, I believe I do. Okay, we should get back to the family now, and I'll try and discreetly ask the question."

"Good luck with that one," Bob mumbled as they turned to enter the café.

Sam didn't respond, although she had the feeling that she would need it, given Mick's reaction so far.

Mick was watching out for them when they reentered the

café. He jumped to his feet and demanded, "Well? What did they say?"

"Let's try and remain calm. Take a seat."

Gertrude rolled her eyes at Sam as if telling her that she'd had a devil of a job getting Mick to do just that in their absence.

"I have a right to know," Mick snapped.

"Dad, please, you're not making this easy." Lee tugged at his father's arm, encouraging him to sit down.

Mick shrugged his son's hand off and fell into his seat. "Get on with it. Time is wasting, and we're eager to begin a search of our own if this mob is too dumb to find her."

"Dad, there's no need for you to be unkind," Tara said, tears welling up again.

"Your daughter talks a lot of sense, Mick. You should listen to her, to both of your children," Sam said. "Getting irate isn't going to help the situation one iota. We're all doing our best to find Patricia, you have no right to judge what has taken place already by the *volunteers* who have tracked across hill and dale to search for your *estranged* wife." *Stick that in your pipe and smoke it, mate.*

"We'll see. I want to know what they've told you. I wouldn't put it past one of the locals to have kidnapped her."

Sam slammed her clenched fist on the table. "That's enough. You have no right to come out with an unjustified accusation like that. We haven't discovered any evidence to suggest such a thing."

"I can believe what I like, and neither you, nor this mob, are going to tell me otherwise. As for evidence, you've got nothing to prove the opposite either, have you?"

This man was winding her up and, frankly, Sam was getting sick to death of it. "Okay, if that's the way you feel about people's efforts so far, I suggest you get out there and see how difficult it really is to find someone presumed missing up on the fell."

"You said the key word, lady, 'presumed'. I will go and search, but I'm telling you this, you and your lot should be knocking on doors around here and seeking out some real answers."

"In your opinion," Sam countered stiffly.

Before she had a chance to ask him what his itinerary had been like the previous day, he announced, "Come on, kids, we're off. I don't think we should waste time here, listening to this nonsense. Sitting around sipping coffee all day long isn't going to find your mother, we will."

"Good luck," Sam called after him. She faced Gertrude whose bottom lip was trembling. "I'm so sorry you had to witness that, Gertrude. Are you all right?"

"I was dealing with all this far better when he wasn't around. Why the dickens did I call him? I can see why Patricia left him, he's a bloody bully. She said as much, but I didn't really believe her. Now I've witnessed it with my own eyes I feel for Tara and Lee, having to put up with his moods on a daily basis. At least Patricia found a way out, but they're stuck with him. Can't you do something about him?"

"Not unless he does something unlawful. All we can do is keep a close eye on him."

Gertrude shook her head. "Isn't this situation stressful enough without a man like that coming here and piling on the pressure?"

"Leave him to us. Try and keep your distance when he's around."

"That's going to be extremely difficult. Enough about him, did the witnesses tell you anything new?"

"No, not really. The two cyclists told us that Patricia seemed to be struggling during the journey, and the one local we spoke to, Jim, told us that he offered her a lift. She had reached the forest by then, and Patricia declined saying she was determined to make it to the end."

Gertrude nodded. "Sounds about right. She is a very determined lady when she puts her mind to it. Did the other cyclists blame me for not sticking with her?"

"I don't think so. You really shouldn't blame yourself."

"But I was the more experienced one. That will prick my conscience for years to come, whether she walks through that door today, next week, or never." Gertrude heaved out a large breath. "My God, my mind has started working over-time now, considering all the possibilities of what could have happened to her."

"You need to stop doing that, otherwise it's going to drive you crazy. I'll tell you something, Patricia isn't the only lady around here with a determined streak."

Bob nodded. "Ain't that the truth? I can vouch for that."

"Thank you, you clearly know the right thing to say when speaking to family members of missing people in this situation."

"Actually, I don't. It's not something I've encountered often. All I can tell you right now is that a proper search party has been organised. Our men should be here soon. We'll get in touch with the local team at Wasdale, see if they can either give us a helping hand or offer an insight into where to look first. The last thing I want you to do is give up hope."

"But if the locals haven't found her yet, what are the chances that you will? They know the terrain and any possible hiding places and have still had negative results."

"I know. We need to look past that for now. I know it's easier said than done but try and remain positive. If Patricia is out there, we'll find her. One thing puzzling me, if I may?"

"Go on. What's that?"

"When you set off, did you leave your car in Calderbridge?"

"That's right. I went back to collect it, and there was no indication that she had returned to it, if that is going to be your next question."

"It was. Your car or hers?"

"Mine. She left hers back in Manchester. Mine's bigger, easier to travel with the bikes hooked on the back, and it's a German make." Gertrude smiled. "I shouldn't have done that, made a joke. I feel guilty now."

"Nonsense. Life is all about finding lighter moments in the face of adversity. Why don't you go back to the hotel and get some rest? Let us know if Patricia turns up, will you?"

"I'll do that. Thank you for what you're doing for us. I realise this must be a difficult case for you to handle, I promise I won't pester you unnecessarily."

"It's fine. I'll give you my number. Ring me if you think of anything I should know or if Mick causes you any problems, and I'll drop by and sort him out."

"You've been so kind, I don't deserve your thoughtfulness."

Sam inclined her head. "Why?"

"If I hadn't been so selfish and left her... she'd still be sitting here with me today." Fresh tears emerged and dripped onto her cheek.

Sam threw an arm around her shoulder. "Honestly, you wouldn't be normal if you didn't have regrets about the situation; however, I'm telling you this for the last time, you need to stop with the recriminations, otherwise it's only going to make you ill."

Gertrude sucked in a deep breath and let it seep out slowly. "I'll try. It's going to be difficult, though."

"I'll see you later, after you've had a good rest. We'll be

here for a while yet. I intend to personally oversee the search."

"Thank you. Patricia would be so grateful to you, and everyone else, if she was aware of the lengths you were all going to, to try and find her."

"We're only doing our jobs. Take care of yourself. See you later."

Gertrude nodded, and with her shoulders slouched and her head down, she strolled to the exit, almost bumping into a woman with a dog coming through the front door.

"I love that this place is dog friendly. Rhys and I must make more of an effort and come for a visit one day soon, with Sonny and Casper, of course. We can have a walk around the lake while we're here, kill two birds and all that."

"You reckon?" Bob replied, totally disinterested.

"Where's your sense of adventure, man? You live in one of the most beautiful parts of the country and yet you rarely get out there to explore it."

"How do you know?"

"I'm sure you would have mentioned it by now. You haven't."

"I'd rather sit at home with my feet up and watch a good movie. Fortunately, Abigail and Milly feel the same way."

Sam shook her head. "Shame on you, all of you, for letting life pass you by like that."

"Hey, each to their own. If we all had the same hobbies life would be extremely boring."

"Mine isn't, that's for sure."

"Neither is mine," he responded adamantly, with no intention of backing down.

. . .

IT TOOK the search team almost two hours to get to The Gather. Sam swallowed down her frustration as she spoke to the officer in charge.

"DS Todd Fairburn, ma'am. Sorry about the delay, it took longer than anticipated to call all the experienced team together."

"You're here now. Do you know the area at all?"

"I've asked around, and a few of the men have been fell-walking over this way a couple of times. I'll be calling on their expertise to lead the way. Still no sign of the missing woman, I take it?"

"Nothing at all. Some of the locals dropped by about half an hour ago, on their way up there again."

"I hope they don't get in our way."

"I'm sure they won't. They've been wonderful so far, so try not to upset anyone. They've done their best to assist, I'd rather not fall out with them."

Fairburn mock-saluted her. "I'll make sure they're treated with utmost respect. Right, anything else we should know before we get on the road?"

"I don't think so. Here's a recent photo I've downloaded from the woman's social media account. Give me your number, and I'll send it to you."

Fairburn did as instructed, and his phone pinged after Sam hit the Send button. "Right, we'll be off then. Are you heading back to Workington or sticking around for the foreseeable?"

"The latter. I'm as much invested in this case now as the locals who have been out there since she was reported missing."

He smiled and marched back to the paddy wagon. Bob came to a standstill alongside Sam, and they watched the van drive off and turn right up the hill to Cold Fell.

"Are we taking bets?" Bob asked.

Sam glanced around to see if anyone had overheard him. "Keep your voice down. No, I have no intention of handing over my hard-earnt money."

A vehicle pulled into the car park, and Mick, Lee and Tara all exited it, slamming the doors behind them.

"Brace yourself for a tongue-lashing, he appears to be in a foul mood," Bob said.

"Follow my lead." Sam turned and walked into the café before the family reached them.

"Oi, don't walk away from me, I want a word with you," Mick shouted.

Sam spun around to face him and patted her hand on her chest. "Are you talking to me?"

"You know damn well I am. Were those your men I saw setting off?"

"They were."

"And what? You're just going to leave them to it, while you sit around here drinking coffee all day long?"

"For your information, I've had two cups of coffee all day."

"And you expect me to believe you, given our surroundings?" he challenged.

Sam smiled. "I don't care if you believe me or not. I'll tell you this, Mr Wolf, I'm not in the habit of lying, and my word has always been my honour." She continued her journey into the café and ordered a black coffee for her and a flat white for Bob. She paid the assistant behind the counter and went in search of a spare table. "Make that three," she called over her shoulder.

Bob chuckled when they sat at the last table at the rear. "Nice one, that told him."

"Did it? Don't look now, but I think he's on his way over here for round two, or should that be round three?"

Bob had his back to Mick and his children and mouthed the word 'Tosser' at her.

"Grade one," she mumbled. "Have you placed your order, Mick? Would you like to join us? I wouldn't mind having a brief chat with you. Our previous time together was very limited."

The two teenagers pulled out a chair on either side of Sam, and their father sat next to Bob, which Sam was relieved about, aware that her partner wouldn't take any unwarranted shit from Mick if he started.

The waitress delivered their drinks promptly.

Sam took a sip of hers and said, "I take it you had no luck up on the fell?"

"It was dreary up there," Tara said. "All I could think about was Mum being missing, alone all this time. What if she's injured, veered off the road on that useless contraption of hers and is clinging to one of the ledges up there?"

"What have I told you about your imagination working overtime, young lady?" Mick chastised his daughter.

"It isn't. I can't help it, Dad. I'm scared. Worried about Mum. You are, too, you just won't admit it."

"I will admit it. I wouldn't have driven all the way up here today if I wasn't concerned for your mother's well-being. What a ridiculous statement to make."

"All right, Dad. Leave it out," Lee jumped in to defend his sister. "Tara is upset, she can do without you having a pop at her."

Sam bashed the table with her fist. "Is all this necessary, Mick? Your children are obviously distraught. All this anger isn't making the situation any easier to deal with."

"It's my way of dealing with things, and I have no intention of altering that either. Where is she?"

"Who?" Sam knew exactly who he was talking about, but

this was her way of letting him know she could be just as obstreperous as him.

"Gertrude. Not only did she leave my wife stranded out there alone in all sorts of weather, she can't even be bothered to hang around, waiting for news."

"Gertrude's exhausted. I suggested she should go back to the hotel and rest while my colleagues carry out the search. I'm advising you not to be too harsh on her and to put your own feelings aside about their relationship for now, for everyone's sake, especially your children's."

"Stop telling me how I should be reacting to this atrocious situation. I'm doing this for them, *her children*, I don't count in this."

"That's admirable of you. I have a few questions I need to ask."

Mick frowned and placed his hands around his cup. "And they are?"

"I wondered what you were up to on Sunday when Gertrude rang you to say Patricia was missing."

"Your information is wrong. She didn't have the decency to ring me until this morning, first thing. The kids and I were just about to leave the house when the phone rang. We dropped everything and came up here. We didn't even have time to pack a bag each. Why?"

"And yesterday?"

"What about it?"

"How did your day pan out?"

"I got up at nine, took Lee to football practice at ten. Then Tara had a dance lesson at eleven. I picked them both up just after twelve, and we went out for a pub lunch because I couldn't be bothered cooking on my day off. Why?"

"It's just a line of enquiry I need to ask, so I can keep all the pieces in order."

"What pieces? Hey, wait a minute, you're not suggesting I

had something to do with her going missing, are you? I was three hours away."

"I'm not suggesting anything of the sort, only getting things straight in my mind."

Lee and Tara both gave their father a confused look. Sam quickly picked up on it.

"Is there something your father isn't telling me, kids?" she probed.

"Leave them out of this. I've told you what you wanted to know, let that be the end of it."

Sam's gaze intensified on Lee and Tara. Their heads dropped, and they avoided eye contact with Sam. She decided to leave that line of questioning for now and possibly have a word with the kids later, when they're on their own.

"Very well. I have a few calls to make, if you'll excuse me." Sam took her cup of coffee with her and climbed the stairs to the Community Room once more.

Bob followed her up to the room.

"Hey, you're not going to allow him to get away with that, are you?"

"With what?"

"Avoiding your questions. If I were in your shoes, I would have thrown the damn book at him. It's plain as day he's hiding something."

"I didn't think it was the right time to push it. I'm going to do some digging of my own before I tackle him again."

"Ah, that makes sense. I had a dreadful thought for a moment there that you were going soft on me."

"Not a cat in hell's chance, matey. Biding my time, that's all. He's a tricky character. We all have to do it now and again, rather than bang our heads against a brick wall."

"I've gotcha. What's next?"

Sam raised a finger and tapped the side of her nose.

"Watch and learn." Then she fished her mobile out of her pocket and dialled the incident room at the station.

Alex answered the phone.

"Alex, I need you to do me a favour ASAP."

"What's that, boss? Do I need to take notes?"

"You do. Got a pen handy?"

"I'm ready."

"Good man. The missing woman's husband and kids have just turned up—that's a lie, they showed up around lunchtime and have been searching for Patricia for a few hours. Anyway, I sense that Mick Wolf is hiding something from me. He's super defensive, but I don't want to push things, not with his teenage children hanging around."

"Okay, so what do you need from me?"

"If I give you his reg, I need you to see if you can track his car through the ANPR system during yesterday afternoon. I need to know if it stayed in the Manchester area or if it travelled up the M6 towards The Lakes."

"Ah, I get where you're coming from. You're ranking him as the prime suspect, am I right?"

"Possibly. I need to dismiss those thoughts, and the only way I can think of doing it is to track his vehicle and see if he's being honest with us."

"Leave it with me, boss. I'll get back to you as soon as I can."

"Appreciate it, Alex. While you check the cameras in the Manchester area, perhaps someone else can check the motorway for me?"

"I'll get Oliver on the case. Don't worry, we'll cover all the angles."

"I know you won't let me down. Speak to you later. Call me as soon as you discover anything."

"That's a promise. How's it going out there?"

"The search team arrived about twenty minutes ago. Hopefully they'll have some news for us before it gets dark."

"Do you suspect foul play, boss? Daft question, of course you do, otherwise you wouldn't have asked me to look into the husband's whereabouts."

"There, you've answered your own question."

"I'll have the answer for you shortly, with any luck. Ta-ta for now."

Sam ended the call with a shake of her head. "That guy… I never know if he's deliberately winding me up or if he just fails to put his brain into gear before asking a question."

Bob laughed. "A mixture of both, I believe. He's harmless enough. A good man, once you get to know him."

"I'm not doubting it, but sometimes, between you and me, he confuses the hell out of me."

"So, you reckon Wolf drove all the way up here after he dropped the kids at home then drove all the way back again, maybe late evening or possibly arriving during the night, without the kids knowing?"

"I know, the timeline is off. He said he was out having Sunday lunch with the kids around the time Patricia went missing."

"That's the only downside I can think of, unless…"

"What?"

"Unless he paid someone to kidnap her or bump her off. Maybe she gave him a rundown of her itinerary and it got him thinking. Maybe he's the type to seek revenge after being dumped."

"The plot thickens, right? We'll see what Alex and Oliver come up with. I hope for the children's sake my assumption is wrong."

CHAPTER 3

*S*am paced the floor for hours, frustration mounting while she waited for the relevant parties to get back to her. She glanced out of the window of the Community Room and saw dusk drawing in.

Bob came up the stairs with a fresh cup of coffee and a slice of homemade chocolate cake for each of them.

Sam shook her head. "It looks yummy, but I think my stomach will reject it as soon as I take a bite, I'm that wound up."

"More for me. My throat thinks it has been cut. They've stopped serving hot food down there, so I thought this would be the next best thing. Dare I ask how long we're going to be around here?"

"For as long as it takes. Have you got a hot date this evening?"

"No, I'm just wondering. I'm bored out of my mind."

"So am I, but that's police work for you."

"I know."

Sam's ears pricked up. Car doors slammed, and there was a lot of commotion going on downstairs. "I'm sensing something is wrong. Come on, let's get down there." She bolted down the stairs two at a time and almost missed the bottom step. Sam saw the paddy wagon on the edge of the parking area, and her heart skipped several beats.

Fairburn raced towards her.

"Well?" she asked.

"We found her, or should I say, her body. A forester was coming to the end of his shift, and something caught his eye. Rather than disturb it, he came looking for a member of the team and took them back to the location."

"Oh God. I hoped this wouldn't be the case. Do we know how she died? Has the pathologist been called?"

"Yes, I've rung him, he's on the way. Reckons he'll be here in an hour. I had a brief look at her, didn't want to get too close for fear of tampering with the scene. I'll say one thing, her neck was sitting at an awkward angle."

Sam ran both hands through her shoulder-length hair. "Damn."

"What's going on here?" Mick demanded as he approached from the road with Lee and Tara.

"Damn," Sam repeated. "Okay, has the scene been cordoned off?"

"It has," Fairburn confirmed.

"Get inside the café, have some refreshments. I'll deal with the family."

Fairburn gestured for the four officers, lingering by the van, to join him, and darted inside The Gather.

"Do I need to keep repeating myself with you, Inspector? If you've got a problem with me then I demand to speak with your senior officer, now."

"I haven't got a problem with you, Mr Wolf. Why don't you all come upstairs?"

"Why? Have you found her?"

"I'll share more details up there. I need to contact

Gertrude at the pub, she should be the first person I speak to."

"What utter bullshit. We're her sodding family, not that bitch."

"Dad, stop it!" Tara screamed.

Lee wrapped his arms around his sister and glared at his father. "Dad, this is so unnecessary. If there's news about Mum, I want to hear it."

Mick turned away and kicked out at a large stone, sending it flying across the car park. "Damn that woman, she'll be the bloody death of me. All right, you win, get her here and order her to make it snappy."

"Bob, will you go and collect Gertrude?" Sam asked.

Her partner set off, and Sam rubbed Tara's arm.

"Are you all right, love?"

"She's fine. Let's get this over with. Up here, I take it?" Mick shoved past and clipped Sam's shoulder.

"Yes. I'll follow you up." Sam watched the family ascend the stairs while a large lump formed in her throat. She wasn't relishing what was about to come. Knew there were going to be fireworks from one particular member of the family.

Bob returned five minutes later with a dishevelled-looking Gertrude by his side.

"What news is there?" Gertrude asked, trying to train her wayward hair, sticking up in every direction.

"Let's join the others upstairs." Sam led the way with Gertrude sandwiched in between her and Bob.

"Oh no," Gertrude muttered after seeing Patricia's family already in the room.

"Please don't worry, stay beside me. I've warned him about keeping his temper under control."

"And you think that will happen?" Gertrude whispered in response.

"I would hope so. Take a seat." Sam glanced up to see the

disgusting way Mick was staring at Gertrude, and it made her stomach flip even more. *You bastard. Is it any wonder your wife left you?*

Lee encouraged his father to sit down, but again, Mick refused to take his son's advice. He crossed his arms instead and tapped his foot.

The two children sat next to each other and held hands.

Sam cleared her throat and stood before the group. "As you know, a search-and-rescue team was arranged, and the men set off a few hours ago. They've recently returned to inform me… that sadly, Patricia's body has been found."

Gertrude sucked in a breath, covered her face with her hands and sobbed.

Mick's gaze shot in her direction. He shook his head and tutted. "Give the woman a bloody Oscar."

Sam ignored him, her attention drawn to Patricia's children. Naturally, they both appeared shocked by the devastating news. Lee hugged his sister who buried her head in his shoulder as she cried.

"I'm sorry for your loss," Sam said, unsure what else to say.

"And what are you going to do about this? How did she die? Where was she found?" Mick shouted, his tone vibrating with anger rather than any other emotion.

"I'm afraid I can't go into specific details at present, not because I don't want to, but I have to see what the pathologist has to say first. He's due to arrive in the next hour. I'll attend the scene with him, and we'll know more then. I'll be sure to let you know as and when I can."

"Is that right? Still intent on keeping us in the dark, I see. I demand to know the name of your senior officer."

"With pleasure. You need to speak to DCI Alan Armstrong. Although he won't tell you any different than I'm telling you. There are procedures to follow when a body has been discovered."

"Was she killed? I demand to know the cause of death," Mick insisted.

Gertrude bounced out of her chair and sprinted across the room to confront him. Bob was the quickest to react. He stood between Gertrude and Mick and held out his arms.

"Come on, don't do this. Think of what this is doing to Lee and Tara."

Sam's heart swelled with pride. It was a rarity for Bob to intervene this way during a confrontation with a family member.

"He needs to keep his trap shut. He has no right being here. Can't you ask him to leave? This situation is stressful enough as it is without him kicking off," Gertrude said before she collapsed into a nearby chair.

Tara left her seat and wrapped an arm around Gertrude's shoulder. "I'm sorry, Dad shouldn't be acting this way. He's still bitter because of the way the marriage ended."

"Don't go there, Tara. You don't have to make excuses for me. I was married to your mother for over twenty years, does that fact not count for anything? She may have fallen out of love with me, but I still loved her." He turned his back on everyone and rested his forehead against the doorframe.

Sam being Sam, went over to check if he was okay. "This is a difficult situation for all of you. It's only going to make things harder if you don't get along. Your children appear to like Gertrude and have accepted her as part of their lives. Can't you do this for them?"

"Why should I? That woman stole my wife and, in the process, ripped my life apart. Why should I simply forgive, forget and move on?"

"This affair affected your children, too. They've found it in their hearts to forgive Gertrude; even now, they're showing kindness that would be far beyond most adults in this situation."

"We raised them well. They're good kids. I'm proud of them. I feel like a knife has been inserted in my gut and it's been torn in an upward jerk, if that makes sense."

"It does. I can totally understand how you must feel. But like I said, you're all in the same boat."

"I can't do it. I just can't. She was my one true love, and now… she's gone." He placed his back against the wall and slid down it to sit on the floor where he cried.

"Dad," Lee called out. He ran to be by his father's side.

Mick hugged him.

Sam took a few steps back, not wishing to intrude on the family's grief a moment longer than necessary. Gertrude and Tara were still wrapped in a firm embrace. In a way, Sam was glad the family had arrived. She would have hated for Gertrude to go through this agony alone. She believed Mick's sour attitude would be relegated to the past now that Patricia had been found.

Bob joined Sam, and they made their way towards the door.

Sam glanced out at the rapidly dimming light. "What a terrible ending, one I never anticipated coming. I had a sense that she would always be found, dazed, concussed somewhere further afield on the fell having veered off route. All of this has come as a shock to me, too."

"Are you all right?" Bob asked.

Sam looked up at him with tears brimming in her eyes and nodded. "I think so."

"Are we going up there now or do we wait for Des to arrive?"

"I think we should head over there in an hour or so, meet him up there. I doubt if he'll know about this place."

Bob glanced over his shoulder at the family and whispered, "Is he still top of the suspect list? Could all this be an act to make you drop your guard?"

Sam followed his gaze and shrugged. "It's far too soon to tell. I'm not ready to dismiss him, not just yet, but we'll keep that between us for now, until we've seen the victim ourselves. Maybe there will be a bunch of clues left by her body that will point us in the direction of the killer."

"Or perhaps that's wishful thinking on your part."

"You're probably right. Come on, let's leave them to it."

She took a first step down the stairs but paused when Mick shouted, "Where are you going? You can't just walk away and leave us."

"I'm not. I thought I would give you some time to grieve. I'll be back soon. I need to get the ball rolling on the investigation."

"To find the killer?"

Sam nodded. "That must remain my priority. I'm going to trust you to all get along now. I think it would be best if you all went back to the hotel soon. I'll need to lock this place up for security reasons once we get on the road."

The family all nodded.

Sam and Bob descended the stairs and entered the café which was about to close.

Emma stood lingering in the doorway, shaking her head. "I can't believe it, Sam. This wasn't the outcome any of us were expecting, was it?"

"No. I'm so sorry, Emma. I know you told me that we could use the room upstairs for a while, did you mean it?"

"Yes, we don't need to set up for the next function until the end of next week. When we opened it up as a venue, I never dreamt it would be used to run a murder investigation. I feel numb just thinking about that. How's Gertrude holding up?"

"I think they're all struggling up there. The friction

61

between Mick and Gertrude appears to have died down, but I'm still a little wary, in case he has second thoughts and starts up again."

"Is it wise to leave them alone, in the same room?" Emma cast an eye in the direction of the door.

"For now. But I'll put in a call for more uniformed officers to attend. Bob and I will be needed up at the crime scene soon, once the pathologist arrives."

Emma shook her head. "I still can't believe this is happening. Not around here. What is the world coming to when a murder happens on our doorstep, in a beautiful location such as this?"

"Try not to think about it, Emma. Hopefully any evidence we find up there will point us in the direction of the killer and all this will be sorted quickly, without too much disruption to the village and its inhabitants."

"I think it's too late for that, Sam. So many people have invested their time trying to find Patricia. Hearing the news that she's been murdered is going to come as a huge shock to them."

Sam peered over her shoulder and then took a step closer to her dear friend. "Have you noticed any of the locals acting suspiciously lately? Heard any possible gossip being spoken over the odd pot of tea?"

Emma's eyes widened. "No way. Not even an inkling. I can't believe anyone from around here would have an evil streak in them that hadn't yet been detected by another local. It's such a small community, we've always had each other's back over the years. You saw how many people took it upon themselves to get out there and search for Patricia, a complete stranger to them. Would that have been the case in another village or even Workington?"

"I admit, you've all been amazing, love. What about any

tourists that have come in this week? Any loners around? Anyone odd that sticks out in your mind?"

Again, Emma paused to deliberate. "Christ, I think you're asking the impossible. The locals coming in here with their friendly banter is a far cry from dealing with a tourist, as you can imagine. It begs the question of whether the killer would have their intentions written on their forehead. Unlikely, right?"

Sam sighed. "Yeah, that's the dilemma we have to deal with on a daily basis. Hard to envisage what someone's motive is likely to have been for killing her."

"Doesn't bear thinking about."

"Don't worry. Are my guys in the way? Are you wanting to shut up shop for the evening?"

"They're fine for another ten to fifteen minutes. Let them have their drinks after all their efforts today. What are your plans?"

"I think I'm going to stick around here tonight. See if they've got a room at the Fox and Hounds."

Emma groaned. "Damn, we have friends and family staying at present, otherwise I'd offer to put you up for a few days. There's a local Airbnb up the road if the pub hasn't got any space for you."

"Don't be sorry. It was kind of you to offer. Any chance I can have a spare key for upstairs?"

"Have the one I gave you for now, just don't lose it. I'll get another couple cut when I find the time to pop into White-haven. I need to pick up a few supplies we're running low on, tomorrow. I could do it then."

"No rush on my part, whatever suits you. I'll be sure to lock it up when we leave for the evening."

"Do you think the family will stick around? He seemed quite feisty, the husband."

"He's calmed down a bit. Not sure if that will change in

the future. I can't see them staying up here for long, although I get the impression that Gertrude will."

"I feel so sorry for her, what she must be going through at this sad time. The guilt is likely to haunt her days and nights for years to come. She pretty much said the same herself when I spoke to her earlier."

"I can imagine. I think she's going to need to give herself a good talking-to or seek out professional advice if she wants to move on. It's going to lay heavy on her shoulders if she doesn't."

Emma nodded. "I'll let you get on; I need to cash up for the evening. Unless your lot want anything else, of course?"

"I doubt it. Don't let us hold you up longer than is necessary, you've been more than obliging as it is."

"Always a pleasure to help out in times such as this. What am I saying? We've never had to deal with anything like this in the community. I'm talking crap as usual, ignore me."

Sam chuckled. "I will. Thanks again, Emma, for putting yourself out for us. Hopefully we won't be in your hair too long. I think it's important for us to stick around and show willing, let the murderer know we're no pushovers, if they're still in the vicinity. Of course, there's every chance they might have moved on by now."

"I hope they haven't, for everyone's sake. They need to be caught, and quickly, and I know what a shit-hot detective you are."

"Thanks for the compliment."

Sam drifted over to where Bob and the other officers were seated at the large table in the centre of the café, close to the cake cabinet with all its delicious offerings on view. The men were in deep conversation about procedures, and Sam decided she'd need to call Rhys, let him know what was going on. She continued over to the window with the ever-changing view of the houses lighting up for the evening on the hillside.

"Hi, it's me. How are you?"

"Fine, what about you?"

"It's been a tiring day. I don't think I'm going to make it home this evening."

"What? You're working through the night at the office?"

"No, I'm out on location, up at Ennerdale Bridge. There's been a murder up here."

"Shit! Really? Who?"

"A female cyclist went missing yesterday, and her body was found in the forest a little while ago."

"Have you caught the person responsible?"

"Not yet, but we will, I'm determined. I'll be staying at the pub here, if they have a spare room."

"What about extra clothes? Want me to pack an overnight bag for you and nip it over? It's not that far, not really."

"Who am I to turn down an offer like that? We could have a meal at the pub before you travel back. It's dog friendly, so bring Sonny and Casper with you."

"Sounds like an excellent idea to me. Do you need an extra suit?"

"Can I trouble you to bring the navy-blue trouser suit and a couple of tops to go with it?"

"And a few days' undies as well?"

"Yes, and my shampoo, deodorant, toothpaste and toothbrush, if that's okay. Oh, and you'd better pack some PJs in case the room isn't en suite."

"Consider it done. I'm nearly home now. I left the office earlier than usual, had a last-minute cancellation. I'll pick up Sonny from Doreen's and take the boys for a walk around the park, then feed them before I set off."

"You're an absolute treasure. Not sure what I did in this life to deserve you."

"Ditto. If you think of anything else you need, send me a text."

"Okay, I'll see you later. I need to travel up to the fell now, see what the pathologist can tell me about the victim."

"Good luck." He blew her a kiss.

Sam ended the call and returned to stand behind Bob. She placed a hand on his shoulder. "We should head up there soon, Des will be here shortly. You know how grumpy he can get if he's held up."

Bob stood and patted the men on either side of him on the shoulder. "Well done on finding her, guys."

"All in a day's work," the youngest officer to Bob's right said.

"Thanks from me, too, men, another job well done."

She and Bob left the table and walked outside the café.

"First, I want to drop by the pub, see if they've got a room for us," Sam said.

"A room? Not sure Abigail and Rhys will be pleased about that."

Sam jabbed him in the stomach with her elbow. "Wise arse. You know what I mean. Are you up for staying overnight? Maybe longer?"

"It depends on who's paying the bill. I can't afford the added expense, not on my salary."

"It'll go down as a business expense, don't worry."

"Does that include meals, too?"

Sam tutted. "Always thinking about that damn stomach of yours. Of course it does."

"In that case, I'd better get on the blower and ring the missus."

"You can talk to her en route."

Bob pointed up the stairs. "Are you forgetting about them?"

"How could I? Why don't you go to the pub? Check if

they've got a couple of spare rooms, and I'll drop my head in and see if they're okay and if they need anything further from us this evening."

Movement at the top of the stairs made her look up. Tara was on her way down, her arm linked through Gertrude's, with her father and brother right behind them.

Sam waited until they reached the bottom and asked, "Are you guys all right?"

"We're going back to the pub," Gertrude said tearfully.

"I was about to suggest the same. We're setting off to see if the pathologist has arrived yet."

"Can we come with you?" Mick asked, his tone subdued.

"I'm sorry, we never allow the general public near a crime scene. I'll keep you informed, I promise."

"Make sure you do." He passed Sam and headed in the direction of the village, with Lee by his side.

Sam nudged Gertrude and asked, "Are you going to be all right?"

"Yes. The family are going back to Manchester in the morning, but I want to stick around, if that's okay with you. I promise I won't get in the way or interfere with the investigation."

"It's your prerogative, I'm fine either way. You have my assurance that we're going to do our very best to try and solve the case swiftly."

"I would hope so. It would be foolish if you didn't. No one wants a killer in their midst, do they?"

"That's true. See you later. Try and get some rest."

"Thank you, Inspector, for everything you've done for us so far."

"Yes, thank you," Tara added, a slight smile tugging at her thin lips.

"You're welcome. I hope I don't let you down." Sam did her best to keep the tiredness from seeping into her voice. It

was getting near the end of her normal working day. It had
started off a harrowing one and had continued throughout
the day for various reasons. All she really wanted to do was
put her head down and rest for twenty minutes, but there
was little hope of achieving such an indulgence with what lay
ahead of her and her partner.

After locking up the Community Room, she reached her
car on the main road just as Bob came around the corner.

"Bad news," he said. "All they had was a twin room available. I took a punt and said it would be okay."

"Shit! Just when I thought this day couldn't get any
worse."

"Thanks, you sure know how to put a dent in a man's
ego."

"Sorry, no offence."

"Plenty taken."

"Rhys is dropping by later with a change of clothing et
cetera. I've invited him to dinner. You're welcome to join us
on one proviso."

"And what's that?"

"You keep your mouth shut about the room we'll be
sharing."

"Hey, as if I'd want something like that getting out. Me
sharing a room with the boss, Christ, that would damage my
reputation in no time at all."

"Cheeky git. Get in the damn car."

"Hey, when do I get to obtain a change of clothes?"

Sam scratched her chin. "Pass. Boss's privilege." She
winked and slid behind the steering wheel.

CHAPTER 4

*S*am impatiently paced the area in front of the forest, flicking her wrist up now and again to check her watch. "Where is he?"

"It's only been ninety minutes, probably rush-hour traffic to contend with somewhere along the route."

Main beam headlights glowed in the distance. A small convoy of vans rounded the bend about half a mile away, and Sam blew out a relieved breath.

"Thank God, they're here at last."

"Maybe not. This route is well known for shortcuts, it might be work vans heading home for the night."

"Maybe you should rethink your opinion," Sam advised.

Bob wrinkled his nose. "Huh?"

Sam averted her gaze and groaned. "Because there's a roadblock at either end of the Fell, numpty."

Bob slapped a hand on his face. "Doh, I forgot about that. It's been an exceptionally long day."

"Yep, and it ain't over yet. It's okay, I won't tell anyone about your screw-up. Your secret is safe with me, pal."

"Are you for real? How magnanimous of you."

Sam heated her fingers with her breath and rubbed them on the lapel of her jacket. "I know, I'm fab, aren't I?"

"That's debatable at times," Bob murmured, disgruntled.

The conversation died down as they both watched the convoy get closer, even though it appeared to be travelling at a snail's pace around the narrow winding road.

"I suppose they're watching out for the sheep," Sam said. "Let's face it, the blighters have a habit of jumping out from the long grass in front of you in the daylight, let alone when the dark settles over the hills."

"Yeah, I noticed. You almost hit that black one around the last bend, somewhere near where the team are now."

"Did I heck? I didn't see it."

"I rest my case."

She slapped his arm. "Bugger off."

It was another agonising few minutes before Des and his team jumped out of their vehicles and began setting up their equipment.

"Suit up, you're slacking, you should have your suits on ready to go," Des reprimanded them.

Embarrassed, Sam mumbled, "Umm... have you got any spares you can lend us?"

"No, because as you know, we never *lend* suits out with the intention of using them a second time. You'll find a couple in the back of my van."

Bob fetched them. Des seemed more pensive than normal to Sam.

"What are you thinking?" she asked.

"That I should be on my way home by now. The wife is going to kill me as I was supposed to be taking my family out to dinner and then the cinema tonight."

"Oh no, so sorry our call has inconvenienced you."

He narrowed his eyes and asked, "Are you? Your tone is coming across anything but sympathetic."

"No, I genuinely meant it. Sorry, it's been a long couple of days or weeks, since my mother's passing."

"How thoughtless of me, of course it has. You have my word I'll go easy on you this evening."

"That'd make a change," Sam responded with a smile.

Bob arrived with the supplies, and he and Sam slipped their suits on and caught up with Des who was halfway between the vehicles and the entrance to the forest, which had been cordoned off. A uniformed officer was standing guard at the tape.

"Ma'am," the officer said, zeroing in on Sam.

"Can you let us through? Do you have a spare torch with you? I don't think I have enough battery left in my phone to guide the way."

The young officer produced a torch from a pocket in his uniform and handed it to Sam.

"I'll give it back to you before we leave. Where's the body located?"

"We've put a trail, using the markers, just inside the gate there, you can't miss it."

Sam smiled her appreciation and led the way with Bob, Des bringing up the rear. She was surprised it didn't take them long to locate the body, considering how many locals had supposedly searched the area before the forest worker had stumbled across the victim's body.

"Penny for them?" Bob asked.

"It's not far from the road. I can't believe her body wasn't found sooner."

"Yep, you took the words out of my mouth. Maybe the locals didn't come through the gate, decided it would be best to stick to the road to search for her instead."

"We were told every inch of the fell had been searched. Clearly, that wasn't the case, otherwise she would have been discovered a lot sooner."

"Hmm... fair point. Wouldn't a local have thought to have searched the forest?" Des asked, equally perplexed by Sam's statement.

"You'd think so. I'm willing to give them the benefit of the doubt. What can we say after them giving up their spare time to help out?"

"If you insist." Des brushed past Sam and shone his own torch on the victim. "My initial assessment is that she's got a broken neck. I'm presuming that's the cause of death and was done deliberately as there are no obvious hazards in close proximity capable of causing such an injury. That's as much as I'm prepared to say at this stage. We're going to need to set up floodlights in the area."

"Do your guys need a hand?" Bob offered.

"No, it's best if we leave it to the experts," Des said. He glanced over his shoulder and saw a member of his team approaching with a couple of large bags in his hands. "Frank, we're going to need the lights up before we go any further. Pronto."

"Leave it with me, boss." Frank delivered the bags, gave one to Des and put the other on the ground a few feet from them.

Unconsciously, Sam began pacing again.

"And you can stop that," Des ordered. "You know how anxious it makes me."

"You spoil all my fun," Sam complained. A cold wind whistled through the trees surrounding them. Rubbing her arms, she said, "That's spooky. Can you please hurry things along so we can get out of here?"

"Hey, I'm not stopping you. In case you haven't noticed,

my team and I have only been on site for five minutes, if that."

"Sorry. Long day, and it's stretching by the minute."

"I know it is. Furthermore, I can do without listening to your whining. It's already getting on my nerves after only three hundred seconds. You can imagine the damage you're likely to cause to my clever mind if I allow you to continue."

"Get you. May I remind you, as the SIO, I have every right to be involved at a crime scene."

"Then you'd be advised not to piss me off, or you and I are going to fall out."

He turned his back on her and took a step towards the victim. Sam pulled a face behind his back, and Bob sniggered. *So much for him going easy on me.* Her eyes widened, and she glared at him, warning him not to drop her in it, but it was too late.

"And you'd be foolish not to believe a man of my intelligence wouldn't have eyes in the back of his head," Des said.

Sam cringed and gulped down the saliva filling her mouth. She glanced at Bob, and he wagged his finger at her.

"And you should listen to your partner's silent advice and keep schtum."

She refused to enter into an argument with him that she was bound to lose. All she needed was a few answers, then they could leave for the evening.

Frank came back with a colleague and set up the lights that instantly lit up the area. At first, the sudden harshness of the beams harmed her tired eyes, but it didn't take long for her to get used to the glare emanating from them.

"Can I move forward?" Sam asked.

"By all means."

Sam bent over the victim to see if she had any other visible injuries. "Is her arm broken, as well as her neck?"

"The right one? Yes, it would appear to be," Des confirmed.

"I wonder if she tried to strike the killer and they used force to get her into the forest."

Des nodded. "It would seem a probable scenario. I'll be able to assess the situation better and tell you more when I get her back to the mortuary."

"What's that?"

Sam's gaze followed to where Bob was pointing at the ground, close to the victim's head.

Snapping a pair of gloves on, Sam took a step to collect the item. "It's one of those army survival knives."

"We'll send it to the lab to get it examined for prints," Des assured them.

"Well spotted, Bob," Sam congratulated her partner. "Old Eagle Eyes strikes again."

"I'm sure Des would have come across it eventually."

Sam circled the victim in the hope of finding yet more clues. If the killer had left the knife lying around, the odds were in their favour that the perpetrator might have left more evidence for them to find. "Nothing as far as I can see."

"I thought you were guilty of raising your hopes unnecessarily," Des said.

The rest of the team arrived.

Des appeared to be put out by their lack of urgency. "Come on, men, make it snappy. We need to get her covered in case these high winds are an indication that the weather is about to change on us. It's more likely to rain up here, isn't it?"

"I was thinking the same," Sam agreed. She took an evidence bag from her pocket, inserted the knife and filled out the label. "Done and dusted. Wait, should I have checked if there was any blood on the blade?"

"Always a good idea in these types of circumstances, Inspector," Des said with clipped sarcasm.

Sam's mobile interrupted the silence a few minutes later. She took a few steps backwards out of respect for the victim and answered the call. "Hey, Crystal, I can't really talk right now. I'm out at a crime scene on the fells. Can I call you back later, from the hotel?"

"Fine. I don't want to hold you up. Where are you, Sam?"

"Up at Ennerdale Bridge. The pathologist has just arrived. I need to go over his initial assessment with him, and then Bob and I will make our way over to the hotel."

"Cosy." Her sister laughed.

"I'm going to ignore that tactless comment. Speak to you later, unless there's something urgent you need to share with me."

"Nope. It can wait. Ring me when you get five minutes alone time. Have fun."

"I won't… have fun, I mean." Sam ended the call and returned to stand alongside her partner. "It was Crystal. I'm going to give her a call back later."

"Everything all right?" Bob asked, concerned.

"I think so. I bet it's about the funeral arrangements. I know she was chasing that up today."

"Ah, yes, seems logical."

It took another ten minutes for the SOCO team to get themselves organised enough so that Des could begin his examination. A marquee had been erected over the victim. Des, Sam and Bob all entered the tent.

"Much better. It was getting rather chilly out there for my liking," Des announced.

"Can we get on with things? Time is marching on," Sam replied, eager to get back to the hotel for various reasons. She glanced at her watch. "Rhys should be arriving soon."

"Far be it for me to hold up your love life when mine has been delayed for the evening," Des snapped.

Sam bit down on her lip and mumbled an apology. "Sorry, I wasn't thinking straight. It's been a stressful few weeks, what with one thing and another."

"No need to apologise. If you held on to your tongue a tad more then you wouldn't get yourself into such mischief, would you? Moving on," he said, not giving Sam the chance to retort. "As initially intimated, she has a broken neck. The bruising around the area would suggest that she was strangled, then her neck was broken as if to make sure death would come swiftly." He opened Patricia's eyelids and nodded. "Yes, there's petechial haemorrhaging, confirming my suspicions."

"Was the knife used at all?" Sam retraced her steps to collect the evidence bag and removed the knife. Bob had to assist her in getting the blade out as it was stiff. "It's clean."

"I can't see any obvious stab wounds or signs of blood anywhere, so that would corroborate your findings."

"Any other visible signs of injuries?" Sam asked.

Des glanced up, gave her one of his 'back off' looks, and she smiled awkwardly at him.

After another five minutes of examining the body, Des rose to his feet. "Nothing as far as I can tell. You may go now and meet up with your fiancé."

Sam's cheeks warmed up under his intense gaze. "Thanks, I appreciate it. I take it you'll be performing the PM in the morning?"

"No, this evening. I'm a professional and deal with things as they come in, less risk of the work building up that way."

That told me. "Okay, I'll look forward to receiving your report either later today or first thing in the morning."

"Probably the latter, but you'll be otherwise engaged, so it shouldn't matter."

"Thanks, Des. I'll be in touch with any queries I may have."

"No doubt you will." He shook out his legs and then went back to study the victim's body from a different angle.

Sam gestured for Bob to leave the tent ahead of her. "See you."

"TTFN," Des replied.

Sam put a finger to her lips and walked back to the car. A few feet later, she said, "I needed to get out of there before his mood escalated. I could sense the tension building between us."

"Hey, I'm not arguing. I was glad to get out of there, I'm bloody starving. Oops... I shouldn't have said that."

Sam laughed. "Why not, if it's the truth?"

THEY ARRIVED BACK at the hotel. Sam collected the key and had a sneaky peak at the room. It was smaller than she thought it would be but it had an en suite, which was a bonus.

When she returned to the pub, she found Bob sitting at the bar, having a pint with Rhys. Sonny whined as soon as he laid eyes on her, and Casper barked. Rhys gently checked their leashes, and Sam rushed over to sit next to her fiancé.

"Thanks for coming and for bringing the dogs with you." She kissed Rhys on the lips and then bent down to kiss each dog on the nose. "Keep the noise down, boys, or you'll have to spend time in the car. Glad you had the sense to sit by the fire, there's a definite chill in the air now."

"I'm not daft." Bob winked. "What do you want to drink?"

"I'll have a gin and tonic, thanks, Bob. How was the trip?" she asked Rhys when Bob departed.

"A nightmare where traffic was concerned, but as soon as

that thinned out, it was fine. What a stunning area, from what I could see of it in the dark."

"It used to be a favourite place to come when I first started walking. It's the reason I fell in love with fellwalking."

"I can understand why. What I can't understand is why we've never brought the dogs out this way."

"Pass. I asked myself the same thing earlier. We can rectify that over the weekend, providing we've wrapped up the case by then."

Bob delivered her drink, and Sam took a large gulp.

"Sorry for being nosey," Bob said, "but you really think this investigation will be completed by then?"

"I can dream," Sam said. "Emma informed me that we can use the room as long as we like, within reason. It's booked at the end of next week. I think we should bring some of the team over, just to have them on hand for when the uniformed officers get pulled back."

"Makes sense. Want me to make some calls now?" Bob asked.

"No, let's leave it until the morning. Can you grab a menu from the bar and check what the specials are, Bob?"

He didn't need asking twice. Bolting out of his seat, he returned in record time, actually skidding to a halt at the table, scaring the dogs who both growled at him. "Damn, I forgot those two are with us."

"Settle down, boys, it's just Uncle Bob playing silly buggers, as usual."

"Bloody cheek." He flipped open the menu and then glanced up at Sam. "Anything and everything an option?"

"Go for it."

"Don't worry about mine, I'll get it on the business, we could get separate bills," Rhys said.

"Are you sure?" Sam felt mean asking him to come all this way and not paying for his dinner.

"Definitely. I fancy a steak."

Bob's hopeful gaze latched on to Sam's. She sighed and rolled her eyes. "Men! Go on then, just a small one in your case," she cautioned her partner.

"Hang on, I've just noticed they've got lasagne on the menu," Rhys said, swiftly sliding the menu across the table to Sam. "Take it away before I change my mind."

"Actually, a lasagne would suit me as well. I hope it's not too big. What do you want, Bob?"

"Go on then, that sounds good to me. It comes with garlic bread and chips, it's a no-brainer."

"I'll go and place the order at the bar. Are you both okay for drinks?" Sam checked with them.

"I'm driving, I'll make this one last the whole evening," Rhys said.

"I should, too, but this one is going down too easily. Bob?"

"I'm torn. Maybe a shot of whisky instead?"

"Okay. Let's get this party started. Is that my bag?" Sam pointed at the holdall on the seat beside Rhys.

"It is, with everything you asked for inside."

"I'll place the order and then take it upstairs to my room."

THEIR MEALS ARRIVED fifteen minutes later, and they all tucked in. Sam was hungrier than she thought she would be and devoured the huge meal around the same time as Rhys and Bob finished theirs. She flattened her hands over her distended stomach. "Oh God, I'm going to regret eating that much this close to bedtime."

"I feel sorry for the dogs." Rhys laughed. "They didn't get a look-in."

"Damn, I forgot they were with us. We didn't hear a peep out of them, the journey must have tired them out."

"That and the fact that I fed them before we left home."

Sam nodded, half an eye on the dessert menu on the blackboard. "Ah yes. That would do it."

"Right, talking of home," Rhys said, "I'd better be thinking about setting off soon. Leave you two to get an earlyish night, so you're fit for work, raring to go, chasing a killer in the morning."

"Shh… keep your voice down, I don't want to make the locals anxious."

"Sorry. I'll finish my pint and go. Can you hold the leads while I nip to the loo? I might as well settle up my tab on the way through."

"Any chance of having some ice cream for afters?" Bob grinned like a teenage kid.

"If you must. None for me, thanks. I pondered about having a pudding, but it was a fleeting thought. I couldn't eat another thing, not even if my life depended on it."

Bob ordered his ice cream at the bar, and Rhys rejoined Sam at the table. They shared an intimate moment together before Bob came back and then left the pub and walked out to the car park where Sam helped settle Casper and Sonny in the back seat. Rhys and Sam shared a hug, and he opened the door and drove off while she stood outside the pub waving until he turned the corner at the top of the road. Sam reluctantly entered the pub again to find Bob tucking into his three scoops of ice cream. She also spotted the Wolf family sitting at a table on the opposite side of the room.

"I'm going to pay the bill and go up to the room. No rush for you to join me, I'm going to catch up with my sister."

"Send Crystal my regards. I'll give you half an hour, how's that?"

"Wonderful." She lowered her voice and added, "Don't get involved if the family start interrogating you about the investigation. Make an excuse and leave, even if you have to dip outside for a breath of fresh air before coming upstairs."

"Okay. I'll avoid eye contact with them and catch up on my social media accounts."

Sam chuckled. "Ever the popular one, eh?"

"I've been known to have my moments. That's shocked you, hasn't it?"

"I refuse to answer in case I incriminate myself. See you soon."

She wound her way up the stairs, pushed the button on her phone that dialled Crystal's number, and then opened the door to her room. After removing her shoes, she stretched out on the bed just as her sister answered.

"I thought you'd forgotten about ringing me."

"Never. Sorry, hectic day. Needed to shove some dinner down my neck and wave Rhys off before I came up to my room."

"Rhys was there?"

"He was kind enough to bring me a change of clothes. What's up? Is this about a date for…"

"Yes. Friday week. I'm presuming you'll be able to get the time off. Poor show if you don't attend your own mother's funeral."

"Why say that? Are you spiky with me because I've left all the arrangements to you and Dad?"

"Amongst other things. Can I remind you that she was my mother, too, and I'm grieving as much as you are?"

"Let it out, Crystal. If you've got something on your mind, let's hear it."

"I haven't." Crystal sighed. "All this has been really hard on me, and I would have much rather have made the decisions with you and Dad, you know how dithery he can be. It's been a nightmare getting any form of decision from him, and you've been totally unreachable at times."

"Anyone would think I've been avoiding you on purpose. I swear I haven't. You're far more organised than me, I would have been hopeless and only got in the way if I'd chipped in with my opinions."

"I guess we'll never know, will we? Everything is arranged now down to the last daisy. That was a joke by the way, there's not a daisy in sight. I hunted halfway around the globe to find some of Mum's favourite flowers, gardenias. They're arriving at my house Thursday next week, hopefully."

"You never cease to amaze me. How's Dad been with all the arrangements?"

"He's left the majority of it to me, still too shocked to get his head around things. He's barely eaten. Vernon keeps cooking extra meals and taking them round to him."

Sam gasped. "I had no idea. I feel even guiltier now."

"Good, so you should. I'm only jesting with you. I know it hit you hard as well, but we needed to get things arranged and out of the way first, before we let the grief consume us."

"I know that now. I regret leaving everything to you. I'm glad you've had Vernon as extra support."

"He loved Mum as much as we did. How's the investigation going?"

"It's only just begun. The real work begins tomorrow, once we have the pathologist's report to hand. You don't want to hear the ins and outs of that. How are you holding up, hon?"

"I'll do my grieving once she's buried. You deal with it how you need to. I'm determined not to let this come between us, Sam."

"Thanks, sis. I do love you and I appreciate what you have done since Mum passed away. It all hit me for six, far more than I anticipated it would."

"Let's get the next week out of the way and move on, love, it's what Mum would have wanted."

"Absolutely. Thanks for being you, Crystal."

"I've got to go. I promised Dad I would drop in with his dinner. Vernon is waiting outside, revving the engine."

"Go, give my love to everyone. See you soon."

"Good luck with the investigation."

The door opened, and Bob entered. He winced and reversed out of the room, but Sam clicked her fingers and beckoned him to come in. She finished her call and placed her mobile on the bedside table.

He sat on the bed next to her. "Sorry, I didn't mean to disturb you."

"You didn't. Everything okay down there, with the family?"

"Yep, they kept their distance, and Gertrude joined them after you came upstairs. They all appeared to be getting on well together."

"United in grief, that was a surprise outcome. I'm going to have a shower and hit the sack. You can put the TV on if you want, it won't disturb me, providing you don't have it too loud."

"I'm not fussed. I doubt if they'll have Sky here. I never watch terrestrial TV, not these days, it's crap."

"I agree. I won't be long."

"How was Crystal?"

"Damn, sorry, she was okay. A bit narked at me for taking a back seat with the arrangements, but I can't blame her. The funeral is going to take place a week on Friday."

"Everyone has different strengths during times of adversity."

She smiled. "I know. Heaven knows how I would have coped if it had all been down to me and Dad. I think I must take after him there, whereas Crystal has Mum's trait of being a good organiser."

"It's wonderful to see that the onus doesn't lie solely on

your shoulders and that Crystal has been there to support both you and your dad."

Sam smiled and nodded, unable to speak because of yet another lump emerging in her throat. She left the bed, walked into the bathroom and ran the shower. Whilst getting undressed she sobbed, grateful the water would deaden the noise of her crying. After believing she was all cried out, grief always had a habit of biting her in the backside.

When will it bloody end? When we finally lay Mum to rest?

CHAPTER 5

The following morning, Bob was chomping at the bit to get downstairs for breakfast, but Sam took her time to get ready, her stomach still full from the fabulous lasagne she'd consumed the night before. She joined him towards the end of his meal and ordered a round of toast that would set her up for what the day ahead had in store for them.

While she waited for the waitress to bring her food, she checked her emails. Disappointment slammed into her stomach at not finding the PM report sitting in her inbox.

"Has it come through yet?" Bob asked between bites.

"Nope. Hopefully it'll pop up within a few hours. We'll have this and get the team organised. I'm thinking of asking Claire, Liam and Oliver to join us."

"That seems overkill. May I ask why?"

"Does it? Now you're causing me to doubt myself. The more we have on site, the easier it's going to be to conduct the house-to-house enquiries."

"What? Tell me you're not intending to question the whole village?"

"All right, I won't. But yes, that's the plan. Do you think it's a dumb idea? Be careful how you answer that, what with me being your senior officer."

He grinned. "I'll answer it truthfully, like I usually do, with sublime tact and diplomacy."

Sam placed a hand to her mouth and said, "Bullshit," into her fist.

"I have my moments."

The waitress delivered her toast and coffee and asked if they needed anything else before she headed back into the kitchen. Sam assured her they had plenty to conquer the day ahead, especially her partner. Halfway through eating her toast, the inner door opened, and the Wolf family took their seats at one of the other tables laid up for breakfast.

"Good morning to all of you. Are you going back to Manchester today?" Sam asked.

"Morning," Mick mumbled. "Yes, as soon as we've eaten our breakfast. How do you think the investigation is going to progress today?"

Sam washed her toast down with coffee before she responded. "I'll be organising my team, bringing most of them out here to conduct the house-to-house enquiries. Hopefully that will give us further insight into which way the investigation should go."

"Do you have any clues or evidence to assist you?"

"Not as such, not yet. I'm still waiting to see what information, if any, the pathologist has gathered from the post-mortem." Sam made sure she kept the knife they had found at the scene a secret, for now.

"When are you likely to find that out?"

"Within a few hours, providing he hasn't been snowed under with more work during the night."

"More bodies to cut open?" Lee asked, excited.

"Do you mind? People are trying to eat," Mick chastised his son.

Bob shoved his almost empty plate away and looked at the remainder of the food in disgust. "It's all right, I've finished anyway."

Gertrude entered the room and hesitated in the doorway. Sam wondered if she was contemplating joining the family for breakfast or sitting at a table on her own. Tara took the decision out of her hands. She left her seat, slipped her arm through Gertrude's and guided her to the seat next to hers.

"It's all right if Gertrude joins us, isn't it, Dad?"

Mick shrugged and kept his gaze glued to his cup. "I guess so."

With interest, Sam watched Mick's hesitation and sudden discomfort come to the fore.

"Are you sure it's okay, Mick?" Gertrude asked, her own reluctance projecting.

"Go for it. If the kids don't mind."

During the rest of her breakfast, Sam sipped at her drink and cast the odd glance in the family's direction. "Are you ready to go?" she asked her partner.

"Yep, nicely replenished and looking forward to the day ahead."

Sam cringed at his choice of words he'd let out in a booming voice as the family all turned their way. She left the table and prodded Bob, urging him to follow her.

Outside, she shook her head at him. "You really need to curb that tongue of yours on occasions."

"What did I say wrong?"

Sam marched in the direction of The Gather. "I'll leave you to figure that one out for yourself."

The café was still shut, and again, Sam was grateful to Emma for supplying her with a key to upstairs. It was coming up to nine. Sam sat at one of the tables and rang the incident room. She had a hunch that Claire would already be at her desk by now. She was right. "Hey, Claire, it's me. We're still here. The body was discovered around dusk last night, in the forest."

"I'm sorry to hear that, boss. What do you need from us?"

"I need three of you to come out here for a few days at least. So, you might need to stop off and pack a bag each before coming out. We've got the use of the Community Room at The Gather. The manager has given us permission to use it until the end of next week."

"Who do you want to join you?"

"You, Liam and Oliver. It's mostly to conduct house-to-house enquiries, but I'd like you to bring one of the spare computers with you. We're still going to need to access the main computer. Will that be possible?"

"Yes, I'll make it work. I'll bring my laptop as well. How exciting, getting the chance to work outside the office for a change and in a stunning location to boot."

"Do you know this area?"

"Oh, yes. I've not been over that way for a little while, but I used to visit regularly when I was a child and in my late teens. My parents were avid walkers, and it was nothing for them to take off for four to five hours, dragging us with them on the seven-mile walk around the lake up there. I have very fond memories of picnicking by the water, admiring the beautiful landscape around us. Hark at me, I lost myself there for a moment or two. Sorry, boss."

Sam laughed. "No need for you to apologise. I totally endorse what you said. This place is in my soul, if that doesn't sound overdramatic."

"It doesn't. There are some places in this world that really do hold a piece of your heart."

"Exactly, I couldn't have put it better myself. Back to

work… We'll expect to see you soon. No, wait, any news on Mick Wolf's car?"

"Nothing untoward. He remained in the area and stopped off briefly to visit someone before he went back to the house with the kids."

"As suspected. Okay, I'm going to feel happier letting them head back to Manchester knowing that."

"Absolutely. I'll get things prepared, and we'll get on the road as soon as Liam shows up."

Sam snuck a peek at her watch; it was five minutes to nine. "I'm sure he'll be there soon."

"Here he is now. Is there anything else you need us to bring?"

"No, we're fine for coffee and food, just bring the computer, and yourselves, of course."

"We're on our way. See you soon."

Sam ended the call, and her gaze was drawn to the panoramic view of the hills all around her. Bob found her a few minutes later, still considering how someone could have the audacity to murder someone in such tranquil surroundings.

Bob perched on one of the tables next to her. "What are you thinking?"

"I'm trying to get my head around what just happened, I suppose. Why would someone choose to take another person's life, up here of all places?"

"I bet you can say that about every location under the sun where a corpse has been found. The difference with this case is that it's personal to you. You know this area like the back of your hand and have always found peace here."

"That's profound of you. I think you're probably right," Sam admitted, which usually went against the grain, admitting he was right.

89

"I've been known to have a good thought now and again. Are the team on their way?"

"Yes, they should be here shortly. Let's get a map of the area, and we'll start planning the routes each of us should take. I'm sure it won't take long to cover the whole of the village."

"What about the outlying areas?" Bob asked.

"We'll get around to them, eventually. Let's concentrate on the immediate vicinity for now."

"Sounds like a plan. The family appears to have accepted the loss of Patricia well, or was that my imagination?"

"I thought the same. I'm glad Tara included Gertrude this morning, she's a very thoughtful young lady, even during her own personal grief. I know from experience how some people go into their shells when a loved one loses their life."

"Hey, don't go getting maudlin on me now. We've got an important investigation to solve, and I need you to be on top form," Bob said.

"Don't worry about me. I had a decent night's sleep once I learned how to switch off from your confounded snoring."

"Yeah, right. That's a likely story."

Sam hitched up an eyebrow. "No story, I'm telling the truth. I even recorded it on my phone."

"Piss off."

Sam removed her phone from her pocket and played the recording. Bob was stunned by the racket filling the room. She stuck her tongue out at him. "Now call me a liar."

Footsteps sounded on the stairs, saving her from him tearing her off a strip for invading his privacy, and a head poked around the doorframe.

It was Emma. "How are things going?"

"We're organising where to begin with our enquiries. I've got three team members arriving shortly."

"Great. If you need anything at all, don't hesitate to ask.

I'll tell the staff to keep you fuelled over the day and to put it on a tab, is that okay?"

"Perfect, thanks so much, Emma. Again, if your staff should overhear anything either amongst the locals or the tourists alike, can you tell them to let us know right away?"

"Consider it done. Do you want a coffee to set you up for the day?"

"That'd be wonderful. Bob will come down and collect them."

"So, I'm the designated gofer, am I?"

Sam grinned, and Emma laughed.

"On that note, I'll leave you to it," Emma said. "Give me five minutes to get the machines warmed up, Bob."

"I'll be down in ten."

THE REST of the team arrived within ninety minutes. Sam was relieved to see them as she was eager to get the investigation underway. She went over the map of the area and the plan she and Bob had pulled together. After that, they left Claire setting up the computer with a fresh cup of coffee and a slice of homemade chocolate cake.

"Blimey, I can see the weight piling on without much effort." Claire sniggered.

"I'm being extra careful," Sam said. "If you get five minutes, pop downstairs and have a gander at what's on offer —or maybe not, it might prove to be too tempting."

"I might give that a miss, for health reasons." Claire chuckled.

"A wise move. Right, come on, gang, we should make a start. You've all got your routes planned out. It should take us three to four hours at the most, providing people are at home when we call."

Claire wished them luck, and they descended the stairs en

masse, separating at the exit of the car park. Liam and Oliver went right, while Sam and Bob went down the hill to the main part of the village. At first, progress was exceedingly slow. Sam stumbled across a few inhabitants who had been involved in the search for Patricia. They had all been shocked to learn the news of her death, and one or two of them even felt pangs of guilt for not finding her sooner. Sam had tried to soothe their injured souls and told them no one was to blame, except for the killer who obviously had an agenda, leaving the body in the forest where it wasn't likely to be found for a few days.

Sam passed Bob a couple of times, and he mumbled words of discontent as he moved on to the next house. She knew this was his least favourite job, and even an outsider could tell it was today, judging by his demeanour.

"Put a smile on your face, man!"

"What? And then sit back and wait for everyone to criticise me for not taking my job seriously enough?"

"As if they'd dare."

"They'd dare, judging by some of the reactions I've got from the locals so far."

"Anything we should be mindful of?"

"Not really, nothing that specific. Personally, I think all this is a waste of time."

Sam stopped walking and reversed to challenge him. "All right, matey, tell me how you'd handle the case, if you think I'm going about it the wrong way."

He wagged a finger. "You're twisting my words; I didn't say that. Look at what we're up against. This place is crawling with tourists, even at this time of the year. Then we've got to get around about two-hundred-plus inhabitants to question… Jesus, we could be out here for weeks, and all I've got with me is the clothes I'm standing in now."

"That's it, make me feel guilty, why don't you? You're

going to feel even worse when I tell you that the others managed to stop off and pick up an overnight bag en route."

He raised his arms and let them drop against his thighs. "That's great! What am I supposed to do? Nip into White-haven and stock up with new gear? And who the hell is going to pay for it when money is so tight at the moment?"

"Can you calm down? I'm sorry, all this didn't happen intentionally. You can take a couple of hours off this after-noon and return home to pick up some clean clothes, if you want."

"If I want? I'd say it's a bloody necessity. Don't forget I'm sharing a room with you. The last thing I need is you taking photos of my undies and pinning them up around the station on every pillar."

Sam's mouth gaped open. After a second, she closed it again and protested, "I'd never do such a degrading thing. I'm shocked you would even think that of me."

"Huh, says the woman who recorded me snoring in my sleep last night."

"Sorry, I apologise for that." She withdrew her phone from her pocket and showed it to him. "Look, I'll delete it."

"I should think so. Shocking behaviour on your part."

"Can we get on with the job in hand now?" Sam glanced up the road and saw Liam and Oliver coming their way. "Can we?"

"Fine by me. What time can I leave, you know, to fetch my clothes?"

Sam tutted. "What if we get this row of houses out of the way first? Then the boys and I can take the next road as there are fewer houses in that one, I believe."

"Sounds like just the ticket." He smiled and pushed open the gate to the next cottage.

That put a bloody smile on your face. It's about time! "Hi, how did it go?" she asked Liam and Oliver when they joined her.

"Nothing to tell at that end of the village, boss. A few of the residents said they lent a hand and were shocked to hear the woman had lost her life, but they couldn't offer any other information."

"Yeah, that sounds familiar. Maybe Bob was on to something after all."

Liam frowned and inclined his head. "What was that?"

"That we could be wasting our time carrying out this task, or words to that effect. The problem is, if we don't, we've got no plan B up our sleeves."

Just then a car drew up alongside them, and a man lowered his window. "I've heard the police are in the village. Do you know where I might be able to locate them?"

Sam flashed her warrant card. "I'm the officer in charge on the current investigation. Is something wrong, sir?"

"Yes, we believe so. My name is Joe Tickle, and this is my wife, Janice." He jabbed his thumb in the direction of the woman sitting in the passenger seat.

Sam peered through the window and smiled at the older woman. "Pleased to meet you both." There was movement in the back seat that caught her eye.

"And this young lady we just rescued from Ennerdale Water. She needs to have a serious chat with you. Go on, Sabrina, tell the nice police lady what you told us."

"Are you all right, Sabrina?" Sam asked. She noticed the young woman's cheeks were wet as if she'd been crying for hours.

"I don't know. It's my friend, Anita, she's gone missing. I've been sat up there for nearly four hours, waiting for her to return. I twisted my ankle in these blasted new boots and I told her to go on ahead. She was desperate for a long walk, to make the most of the good weather before the rainy season and winter gales set in up here. These nice people offered to give me a lift. I would have

TO CATCH A KILLER

contacted The Gather, knowing that you were temporarily based up there, but my reception was non-existent on my phone. Is there any chance you can help me look for her, perhaps set up a search party, something along those lines?"

"We can definitely organise something for you. Is she an expert hiker or novice?"

"I'd put her somewhere in the middle, going towards the expert end of the scale."

"Why don't you come with me to The Gather? I have a member of my team over there permanently, at present, while the rest of us are out here, conducting house-to-house enquiries. I can leave the guys to get on with the task I was involved with and come back with you. There, I can make the necessary arrangements for another search party. I'm sure the locals will do their best to get involved."

"Thank you, thank you, thank you for taking me seriously." She placed her hands on the shoulders of the two people in front of her. "Joe and Janice, I can't thank you enough for the kindness you've shown me. Anita enforced upon me what a wonderful community this was."

Sam helped the young woman out of the car and shouted for Liam to assist her. "Liam, can you lend a hand here, please? Sabrina has turned her ankle badly. I need to get her back to the hub at The Gather."

Liam grinned. "Are you up for me carrying you?"

"I'm around nine and a half stone," Sabrina said, her cheeks reddening.

"That'll be a breeze." He opened the car door and helped her to get on her feet and then swooped and lifted her effortlessly into his arms. "There, you're as light as a soufflé, if that's the right saying?"

Sam laughed. "It's not, but I kind of prefer your version to the original one."

"I do, too," Sabrina said. Without prompting, she looped her arms around his neck.

"Guys, you carry on. I need to have a chat with Sabrina here. I'll rejoin you soon, hopefully," Sam called over to Bob and Oliver.

Bob gave her the thumbs-up. "No hanging around up there for a bacon roll either, Liam."

"As if I would, boss."

They returned swiftly to The Gather. Sam was surprised by Liam's dexterity with the extra weight he was carrying. Although she would never have dreamt of saying that out loud.

Claire looked up, stunned to see them back so soon, and pulled a chair out next to her desk for Liam to lower the injured Sabrina in.

"Can we get you a drink or something to eat, Sabrina?" Liam asked once he'd placed her gently into the chair.

"A coffee, no, maybe a herbal tea would be better, if that's okay with you?"

"I'll see what they've got on offer. Anyone else fancy anything?"

"No, we're both good," Sam replied.

Liam left them, and Sam gave a brief assessment of what Sabrina had told her about Anita going missing up at the lake.

"Do you want me to get onto the station, try and get another team out here, boss?"

"If you would, Claire. The sooner we get that particular ball rolling, the better. All right if I ask you a few extra questions, Sabrina? Are you up for that?"

"Yes, I think so. Although I have to say, I'm not sure what else I can add."

"We'll give it a go, eh?"

Liam reappeared with a cup of tea and a slice of cake for Sabrina. "I took a punt that you'd need more than a cuppa."

"Thoughtful of you, Liam." Sam smiled. "Thanks. Now, can you get back out there again with the others?"

"On my way."

"Thank you again for your kindness," Sabrina called after him.

Sam glanced around the room and then walked towards the map of Ennerdale Water on one of the walls. "Am I right in thinking you were probably somewhere on this side of the lake?"

Sabrina tore off a piece of her Victoria sponge and held it close to her mouth. She nodded. "Yes, over to the right. We'd walked past the bridge and were fifteen minutes or so along the track on the right-hand side of the lake. The ground is very uneven there, boggy in parts because of the recent rain. I was busy talking to Anita and forgot to keep an eye on where I was stepping. She had me enthralled, telling me tales of what she'd encountered in the area over the years."

"Is Anita a local?"

"No, but she's visited the area dozens of times. It's one of her favourite walks. That's why I'm so surprised she's gone missing; she knows this area inside out. It doesn't make sense." Tears welled up.

"Try not to get upset. Claire, you get on to the station, see if you can get the team back here quick smart. I'm going to nip downstairs and ask Emma to rally the locals, see if they're up to giving us a hand. You have your drink and eat your cake in peace, for now, Sabrina. We're going to need to get your ankle seen to as well. I'll ask Emma if there's a doctor in the village who we can call upon."

Sam ventured downstairs and into the café where she bumped into Gertrude.

"How are the interviews going with the locals, Inspector?"

"My team are still out there, knocking on doors. I have to say, the response we've had so far has proved to be disappointing. What are you up to?" Sam ran an inquisitive eye over the cycling gear Gertrude was wearing.

"I need to get out there, feel the wind in my hair and the ache in my muscles."

"I understand. Did the Wolfs get on the road okay?"

"Yes, they left straight after breakfast. I believe our relationship is back on track, for now, at least. Who's to say what lies around the corner, once we start making the funeral arrangements?"

"Keep positive, it might all go off without a hitch."

"I'm hoping that you'll have some positive news for us by then and that you will have caught the person who did this to Patricia."

"We're doing our absolute best. Will you excuse me...? I need to have a quick chat with Emma while she's free." Sam stopped short of telling her about Anita going missing, aware how unnerving that might be for Gertrude, hearing the unexpected news.

"Of course. It is time I got on the road, anyway. Good luck, you know where to find me if you need to ask me any questions or if you have any news for me."

"I do. Enjoy your ride. Well, as much as you can in the circumstances." Sam smiled and watched Gertrude walk out of the door. She sighed and continued on her mission, a sudden lump clogging up her throat.

Emma was dealing with various invoices when she walked in. "Knock, knock, can I come in or am I disturbing you?"

"Not at all. Take a seat. Shove those invoices on the desk, I'm in sorting-out mode. How's it going out there?"

"Nothing much to report regarding the Patricia case,

however, something else has come to my attention that I'm hoping you can lend a hand with."

"Okay, you've got my undivided attention. What's up?"

"We've got a lady upstairs who was hiking with a friend around the lake. Unfortunately, Sabrina twisted her ankle and was unable to complete the walk. She insisted her friend continue on the route while she rested. After four hours, Anita hadn't returned. A couple passed Sabrina and offered to give her a lift back to the village. First of all, I wondered if there was a doctor in the village who could take a look at her ankle."

"I have a friend who is a retired nurse, how about I give her a call? If the injury isn't that bad."

"It isn't, at least I don't think it is. That would be fabulous if you can arrange that for me. Also, and this is another big ask, can you rally the locals again, see if they'll lend a hand searching for Anita?"

"Let me get that organised ASAP." Emma picked up the phone. "Hi, Jack, it's Emma. Sorry to have to put this on your shoulders again so soon, but is there any chance you can pull the locals together and set up another search party? Yes… that's fabulous. Different location this time. It'll be around the lake. A young lady has failed to return after four hours, and her friend is very worried about her… marvellous, I'll let the SIO know. Speak to you later." She ended the call and smiled. "I knew he wouldn't let me down. He's going to make a few calls. He's the chief organiser and the one we most rely on to get things actioned. Now all I have to do is ring Rita, see if she's around today."

"Thanks, Emma. I'm blown away by your resourcefulness."

"Get away with you, it's been a pleasure to help out, not that I've done much, not really. Right, here's the number. Let me give her a call."

"I'll nip to the loo, be back in a second or two." Sam left Emma to it and returned to the shop area of the café.

She spent a penny, and Emma joined her in the giftware section, displaying all the wares created by talented locals.

"Some of this stuff is amazing," Sam said. "I must take a closer look before we leave, *if we leave*. Still, that's no great hardship for me, it's wonderful being back here."

"So glad to be catching up with you again after all these years, even if it is in such dire circumstances. Rita's on her way. She used to be the district nurse for a few of the villages around here."

"Great news. I don't think it's too serious. Right, I'd better get back upstairs, see if Claire has had any joy getting a team to come and join us again. They'll be sick of this place soon. Nah, what am I saying? You'd have to be an idiot to get sick of this area. See you later."

Upstairs, Sabrina had finished off her cake and was taking the last sip of tea. Claire was chatting to her, making her feel at ease.

"Any news?" Sam asked.

"Yes, they're on their way back, said to give them an hour or so."

Sam sank into one of the spare chairs and let out a weary sigh. "That's a relief. Emma has managed to get in touch with the local team leader, so all is good there, and she also rang a retired district nurse who is on her way to tend to your injury, Sabrina. Better than going to A and E, although it might come to that if there's something more sinister going on than just a sprain."

"I don't think so. I'm making sure I keep my boots on. The support around the ankle might be giving me a false impression, though, and it might turn out to be worse than I first feared."

"Either way, we'll find out soon. So, with everything now

in hand, I need you to chill, keep the weight off your feet, and try to remain positive. The area will be flooded with people soon enough, all searching for Anita. We'll find her."

"I hope I don't end up with egg on my face and she walks into the café as though nothing has happened."

"For her sake, I hope she does, but I understand what you mean."

Footsteps sounded on the stairs, and a slim, grey-haired woman arrived. "Hello, I'm Rita. Is Sam around?"

Sam leapt to her feet and crossed the room. "That's me. Thanks for coming, Rita. This is Sabrina. She seems to think it's a bad sprain, but I'd rather err on the side of caution."

"I'll soon tell you. All right if I examine her here? I've brought my bag of supplies with me."

"Do you need some privacy? Claire and I can go else-where for ten or fifteen minutes."

Sabrina shook her head. "I'm okay with you sticking around."

"That's sorted then. Let's see what we've got going on here." Rita put her bag on the floor beside Sabrina while the young lady tentatively removed her boot. "Gently does it now."

Once Sabrina had removed her boot and her thick sock, the bruising she revealed caused Sam to wince and suck in a breath. "Ouch, that looks really painful."

"This might be a case of it looking worse than it actually is. Do you tend to bruise easily, Sabrina?"

"Yes, I was prone to falling over a lot as a youngster and used to be covered head to toe, black and blue, most days." She prodded her ankle. "It doesn't feel too bad."

"The telling time is when you try to walk on it again, without the support of your rigid boot around the ankle," Sam suggested.

"One thing at a time," Rita warned. "Let me examine it

thoroughly first. Does that hurt?" She pressed incrementally around the ankle at the fleshier parts.

"Ouch, the last part you touched hurt quite badly."

"Okay, Sam, would you give me a hand to get Sabrina up on her feet?"

Sam took a few steps forward and helped to ease Sabrina to her feet with Rita holding her on the other side.

"Let's see how you go. Walk towards the door if you will?"

Sabrina took a few tentative steps, however, the effort proved to put too much strain on her ankle, and it gave way on her again.

"That's not good. We might need to get you to A and E after all, just as a precaution. I think a ligament might be torn or you might even have chipped a bone in either your ankle or foot. We won't know which until an X-ray has been taken."

Sabrina teared up again. "I can't. I really don't want to leave without Anita. Will it damage it even more if I delay going to the hospital?"

"It might do, if you continue to use it. On the other hand, if you keep it rested then I'm sure you'll get away with it, at least until tomorrow. The choice is yours."

"I'd like to remain here, just until I hear news that my friend has been found safe and well."

"That's your call," Rita said. She got to her feet and picked up her bag.

"Can you not strap it up as a precaution?" Sam asked with an accompanying smile to cover her astonishment.

"I could. Do you think you'd be more comfortable that way?" Rita asked Sabrina.

Sabrina's gaze flicked between Sam and Rita. "We can try, if you think it'll do any good."

"We won't know until we give it a go." Rita opened her

bag and removed a small bandage which she unfastened and wrapped around Sabrina's ankle.

Sabrina flinched several times until the bandage was secured.

"I'll leave you my number in case you need me to examine it further."

"Thank you. It feels pretty tight, but no pain no gain, isn't that what they say?"

CHAPTER 6

Sam peered out at the night sky, disappointment clouding her every thought.

"Penny for them?" Bob said from behind her.

He was sitting up in his bed, still wearing the same clothes. His planned trip home had been unavoidably postponed due to them getting involved in the search for Anita Davila.

"Where can she be, Bob? And what the fuck is going on here?"

"God, if only we knew the answers to both of those not-so-simple questions, I think we'd be millionaires, sunning ourselves on a couple of swanky yachts, island hopping in the Caribbean."

She smiled and walked back to her single bed. "It would be lovely to dream of getting away from all these blasted serial killers we seem to be chasing day in, day out. Why the heck is the world so angry right now?"

"I'm with you on that. Abigail had to call her friend the other day to get herself out of a sticky situation."

"Oh, what was that all about?"

"A car suddenly stopped in front of her and turned right, failed to use the indicator. Abigail had to brake sharply, fearing she might go into the back of this damned Volvo. She blasted her horn and then drove home, or tried to."

Sam frowned. "Why? What happened?"

"She got five hundred yards up the road and then looked in her rear-view mirror to see this sodding Volvo behind her, flashing its lights and beeping its horn at her."

"Never. What the fuck is wrong with people? She didn't stop, did she?"

"Not likely. Anyway, she drove around the roundabout, near the dual track, and this car started to move out behind her, as if going to overtake her. Her heart in her mouth, she floored the accelerator and left the car behind. I've been giving her lessons about using evasive tactics when needed."

"I bet you have. So, did the driver turn around?" Sam wriggled forward to the edge of the bed as he continued to tell her his heart-pumping tale.

"Did they heck. Unfortunately, Abigail got snarled up in the traffic ahead of her. It slowed her down, allowing the driver to get on her tail again, beeping the horn, flashing the lights."

"Jesus, that's insane. I bet there wasn't a copper around either, not when she really needed one. That's harassment or road rage. Does she have a dashcam in the car?"

"Not at the time. I've since nipped into Halfords to purchase one, which I had planned to set up for her this weekend. Anyway, Abigail tried to lose the driver several times. On that stretch of the road there's no way she could have overtaken the car in front, otherwise she would have done. The driver was relentless. She tried ringing me, but I think we were busy and I had put the phone on silent, so I wasn't aware she'd rung until I checked my messages that night. I was seething on her behalf."

"I bet. I don't suppose she had a chance to take down the car's registration, did she?"

"No, it was too close for her to see. After travelling ten miles and this chump tailgating her closely all that way, she'd had enough and finally called her friend, Kath, who lived close to where they were heading. Without hesitation, Kath jumped in her car and headed towards Abigail. When she spotted her, she turned around and followed the other car. She instructed Abigail to pull into the lay-by near our house, glad she didn't lead the nutter home. Who knows what the bastard would have got up to?"

"Quite right, always good to have a diversion tactic to hand. Wait, you said this went on for ten miles. That's bloody ridiculous. That driver must have been loopy, all because Abigail blasted her horn at them? Beggars belief, doesn't it? I'm dying to hear the outcome; I would have been going frantic by now."

"Abigail said she was having trouble holding on to the steering wheel as her hands were so slippery. Anyway, she pulled into this lay-by, in front of a lorry, and the car slowed down alongside her, but Kath forced the driver on, refusing to let the driver get out of the car. They drove around the corner, allowing Abigail the time to reverse and shoot back to our house; our road was a stone's throw away. Abigail sat there shocked until Kath drove up. Her friend jumped out of the car, hugged her and said, 'You'll never guess what.'"

"What?" Sam asked, not in the mood for a guessing game.

"'It was a bloody woman,' Kath said."

Sam's head jutted forward. "No way. What the actual fuck? Did Kath speak to her? Tell me she didn't confront her."

He rolled his eyes. "Kath told Abigail not to mention this to me, but Abigail took no notice. Kath showed the driver a fake badge she carries around with her, just in case."

Sam's mouth dropped open and then closed again. "She doesn't! Well, I never. And?"

"Apparently, Kath got out of her car and approached the driver who lowered her window and had her phone in her hand. The driver said, 'I'm filming you, I'm going to show this to the police.' Well, Kath nearly pissed herself laughing at the driver's audacity. Her face was a picture when Kath produced her fake ID."

Sam tipped back on the bed and laughed until her sides hurt. "Oh God, what a bloody nightmare. It was all good come the end, but it could have turned out so differently."

"I know, it doesn't bear thinking about. Kath warned the driver that there would be a ticket coming her way soon for road rage and nearly causing an accident. The damn woman started crying. Kath asked her why she did it, and the driver blamed Abigail for nearly bashing into the rear of her."

Sam sat upright on the bed once more. "What a twisted bitch. She should be on a psych wing in the nearest hospital, not behind the wheel of a car. She's a danger on the road."

"Exactly. Abigail was still really shaken up several hours later when I got home."

"Bless her, it's enough to put someone off driving. Give her a hug from me when you next see her. Sorry you didn't get to go home and pick up your extra clothes today. Why don't you rinse your pants out in the bathroom? They should dry overnight or when the heating comes on in the morning."

"I'll pass and go commando. I've done it before during an emergency."

Sam pulled a face and shook her head. "Not whilst working alongside me, I hope?"

"I couldn't possibly comment."

"Eww... that means yes."

"Are we eating tonight?" Bob swiftly changed the subject.

"You can, I don't think I could stomach anything. I was planning on making a few notes regarding the two cases. I didn't tell you, I got confronted by Gertrude on the way back here this evening. She was on her way out again on her bike, for another mind-clearing ride."

"Right, what did she confront you about? Or is that a dumb question?"

"Probably, but I'm used to them from you. No, in all seriousness, she must have heard about Anita from the locals and had a pop at me for pushing Patricia's case aside to deal with the new one."

"Bloody hell, that's ridiculous, we've done no such thing. And what happens if the cases are linked? We don't know any different at this stage of the game, do we?"

"Precisely. I know it was the grief talking but I'd like to think she'd see that we were doing our very best for her, for Sabrina and for the community by setting up an incident room here."

"No pleasing some folk. Although, I can kind of see where she's coming from, in a way. Right, I'll be back soon. Want me to bring you back some cheesecake? It's exceptional here."

"And how do you know?"

He grinned and fastened his shoelaces. "I'm off. Want some or not?"

"Not, but thanks for offering."

As soon as he left the room, Sam placed her pillows against the headboard and picked up her mobile. She checked in with Rhys before she got back to work. "It's me. How are things?"

"Hi, I've been thinking about you all day. We're fine. How's the investigation going?"

"It's not, not really. We've had to conduct another search today for another missing tourist."

"Heck, that's not good, Sam. What the dickens is going on up there?"

"If I knew that, I wouldn't still be here, I'd be at home, snuggled up to you."

"Sorry, I didn't mean to ask the obvious."

"No, it should be me apologising for snapping at you."

"It's been a stressful day for you. Have the locals been helping you search?"

"Yes, bless them. Our team have been out there, too, lending a hand. It's perplexing how these women keep going missing in a small village such as this."

"But it's a tourist area, nonetheless, hon."

"I'm aware of that. Okay, I need to go and grab something to eat now. I'll speak to you tomorrow, love you." Sam ended the call, not giving him the chance to reply, and then felt ten times worse. *I'll give him a bell later to apologise.* Needing comfort food, she changed her mind about having dinner, picked up her notebook and pen and headed downstairs to sit with Bob.

He was already tucking into a starter of garlic prawns. "Hey, have you changed your mind? Let me get you a menu."

"Sit there, that's an order. I'm quite capable of looking after myself. What are you having for your main meal?"

"Steak and Guinness pie and chips."

"Sounds delicious, I might have the same. Do you want another drink?"

"I'll have half, need to keep my wits about me for work tomorrow. I've got a tyrant of a boss…"

She pointed and narrowed her eyes. "Watch it, matey."

He laughed.

She placed her order at the bar and returned with their drinks to sit with him while they waited for their meals to arrive.

He pushed his starter plate away and lifted his glass. "That was passable."

"What? Are you having a laugh? You ate every scrap of it. Don't let the staff hear you say that, they're not likely to understand your sense of humour. I struggle with it at the best of times."

He grinned. "Whatever. Hey, passable is good in my book."

Sam shook her head and sipped her drink. "You're incorrigible. Are you up to doing some brainstorming over dinner, or would you rather leave it until the morning?"

"Is that a genuine question? Because by the look of it, I'm not going to have a lot of choice."

Sam twisted her pen and stroked her notebook. "Ah yes, I see what you're getting at. We can leave it, no pressure from me."

"No, I'm fine. What's on your mind?"

"One murder and a missing person, what's on yours?"

"Smartarse."

"I've been called worse. The thing is, we're not sure yet if the two cases are linked, so we really should be dealing with them as if they're two separate investigations, unless we discover any evidence to the contrary."

"Definitely makes sense to me. Hopefully, when the search begins again at first light, Anita will be found, safe and well."

Sam tutted. "I have my doubts. There's a niggling feeling in my stomach, telling me the cases should be linked. Let's hope Anita's body doesn't show up around the lake; that's going to be enough to link the two cases."

"Where's your PMA gone?"

"It's on strike, off with the fairies at the moment."

Bob's main course arrived. The aroma caused Sam's stomach to rumble noisily.

"I can't believe you were willing to give dinner a miss tonight. Listen to your body, it's telling you what a mistake that would have been."

"All right, enough of the lectures, I've placed an order now. I think I'll pinch a chip in the meantime."

He picked up his fork and went to jab her with it. "You dare!"

"But I'm your senior officer, you have to give me one."

He raised his fist and smiled. "Oh, I'll give you one all right, if you come an inch closer to my plate."

The waiter arrived with Sam's dinner, putting an end to their little spat. Calmness descended between them, and Sam polished off her plate of food in record time. "I guess I was hungrier than I thought."

"Now we can discuss the cases."

"Not sure I want to now I've eaten a huge meal. I'm going back to the room, to try and focus on the investigation there."

"You should learn to give yourself a break, Sam. We've been at it non-stop all day. Neither of us took time out for lunch, did we?"

"All right, if you say so." Instead of listening to his advice, she flipped open her notebook.

He groaned. "I give up."

"I should, you won't win. You should know that by now."

"I do. If we're going to link the investigations, what do we have? Both victims—it doesn't feel right calling Anita a victim if we don't know what's happened to her."

"There in lies my dilemma. Nope, I'm making an executive decision, we're going to have to treat both cases as individual ones, at least until Anita is found."

"Fancy a pudding?"

"You mentioned cheesecake earlier, I think that was what tempted me down here in the first place."

"I'm going to have a sticky toffee pudding, not had one of those in ages."

Bob left his seat to place the order at the bar. Sabrina walked in, appearing hesitant in the doorway. Sam gave her a brief wave and then regretted it when Sabrina came towards her.

"Oh, hi. I'm a bit out of my comfort zone, coming in here by myself."

"You're welcome to join us. We won't be stopping long, though. How's the ankle?"

"Better now I've got used to it being strapped up. I'll sit over here, within spitting distance of you, if that's okay?"

"Of course it is."

Sabrina gingerly lowered herself onto the bench seat a few feet away from their table. "I take it they've called off the search for the evening?"

"They have, there's no point risking more lives out there. The terrain can be a bit rugged in certain areas along the path, as you know."

Sabrina nodded. "Only too well. Be honest with me, what are the odds of her being found?"

"Hey, don't even go there. There's every chance of that happening. You need to remain positive at all times. There are so many variables we need to consider about her disap-pearance. For all we know, she might be lying out there, having taken a fall, concussed after bashing her head on a rock or something similar."

"It's the not knowing that is tearing me apart. Will the search begin again first thing?"

"It will. Probably at around eight when the light is on their side. Shall I get you a menu?"

"Thank you, that's so kind of you."

Sam left her seat, collected a menu from the bar and

handed it to Sabrina. "Let me know what you fancy, and I'll place the order for you."

"Again, I appreciate your assistance, I feel so incapacitated with this damn ankle of mine."

"I'm sure it'll heal quickly. I don't think I've asked you yet, where are you from?"

"Bristol, or thereabouts, on the outskirts."

"Ah, nice area, I've visited it a few times. How long have you been coming to The Lakes?"

"Only the last couple of years, but Anita visits a few times each year. She's always said she wanted to move up here, but the price of property is horrendous, especially in the areas she would have preferred to have lived."

"Where's that?"

"Keswick, around there."

"Lovely part of the world, but as you say, it's very pricey. What does Anita do for a living?"

"She's an entrepreneur. Don't ask what she does exactly, because I couldn't really tell you. Money is coming in all the time, she's very busy, a workaholic, and it's paid off over the years."

"I should have asked all of this earlier but I wanted to get the search underway at the earliest opportunity, what with the fading light about to hit us."

"It sounds logical to me." She opened the menu and closed it again. "I wouldn't know where to begin."

"I had the steak and Guinness pie, it was delicious, not too filling, not like some pies I've had over the years."

"Okay, you've helped me out yet again."

Sabrina went to stand, but Sam insisted Sabrina stay put. "Don't worry, I'll order it. What do you want to drink?"

"An Appletiser, if they have one. Let me give you the money."

"Don't worry, we can sort that out afterwards."

Sam put the order in and then retook her seat.

Bob reappeared from the toilet and sat opposite her.

"What about Anita's family? Is she married?"

"No, she's got a really dishy boyfriend—don't tell her I said that. He's a pilot and French."

"Nice. Is he aware of the situation?"

"Yes, I rang him. He's asked me to keep him informed. He has a super busy schedule and unfortunately can't make it, not for a few days."

"Hopefully we'll have found her by then. What about her family? I'm assuming you've informed them."

"Yes, her mother, Rachel, is coming up in the morning. She had an appointment with the oncologist today that she couldn't postpone."

"Oh no, I hope it's not bad news?"

"No, thankfully she's in remission from breast cancer."

"Glad to hear it. Cancer sucks, it's far too prevalent these days."

"Yes, my father died of it last year. It was horrendous watching him suffer come the end, the disease eating away at him."

"So sorry to hear that." A sudden bout of grief overwhelmed Sam.

Bob nudged her knee with his under the table, snapping her out of it. She smiled to reassure him that all was hunkydory in her world.

"Let's hope that we have good news to share with Rachel when she arrives. Any idea what time that will be?"

"Towards lunchtime, I think."

"That gives the search teams around three to four hours in the morning to find her."

The waiter arrived with Sabrina's food.

"We're going to leave you now. Enjoy your meal. Don't worry, I've taken care of the bill."

"Oh no, now I'm going to feel guilty eating it."

Sam laughed. "Nonsense. Not me personally, this one is on the Cumbria Constabulary, it's the least we can do."

"Thank you, you're very kind."

Sam smiled and left the bar with Bob. They entered the bedroom, and Sam immediately withdrew her notebook and pen.

"Right, where were we?"

Bob puffed out his cheeks and collapsed onto his bed. "Do we have to? I'm cream-crackered and could do with some rest. It's not like we haven't gone over things a thousand times already."

Sam sighed; he had a valid point. She slammed her notebook shut and dropped it on the table beside her. "You're right, we'd just be banging our heads against a bloody wall. I need to give Rhys a call, I was a bit off with him before I came downstairs for dinner."

"You do that while I grab a quick shower, that way, at least you'll know I'm clean, even though my clothes are manky."

She laughed. "Why don't you head home first thing in the morning?"

"Because we've got a young lady to find. Once she's been located then, and only then, will I consider deserting my post."

"You'll hardly be doing that, but I appreciate your gesture."

"I'm a decent chap, even if you have a habit of forgetting that at times." He ran into the bathroom when she reached for her pillow.

"Cheeky shit!" she called after him.

"I can't hear you, I've got the shower running."

"Whatever," Sam shouted back. "You still have to face me when you come out." She smiled and picked up her phone.

She didn't get the chance to ring Rhys because he beat her to it. "Hey, I was just this second going to ring you."

"Thought I'd save you the bother. Did you enjoy your meal?"

"It was delicious. That's me stuffed and ready for bed now." The noise of the shower filled the room; she had to think quickly on her feet. "I'm running the shower, it's not always hot, so this will have to be a brief one."

"It's fine. Want me to give you a call back?"

"No, I'll be flat out when I've had my shower, it's been another traumatic day. I miss you."

"I was just about to say the same, and so do the boys, especially Sonny. He's wandering around like a lost soul at the moment. Keeps putting his paws up on the windowsill, watching out for you."

Sam welled up. "I've never been away from him this long before. He'll think I've run off and left him."

Rhys laughed. "Hardly. I'll make sure he gets plenty of cuddles in your absence."

"You're amazing. I'm sorry for being so snappy with you earlier."

"You have nothing to be sorry about. How's it going there?"

"We have yet another missing person to find."

"I feel for you. Can't wait to have you home with us again, so that we can plan our next adventure with the dogs."

"You're nuts, which is why I love you. I'm going to have to go now. I'll give you a ring tomorrow."

"I'll keep my fingers and toes crossed that the missing person shows up and that you're back with us soon. The dogs aren't the only ones missing their cuddles."

"Ditto. Love you, Rhys. Thank you for being you."

"Who else would I be?"

"You know what I mean. You're a breath of fresh air, compared to…"

"Your last beau, shall we call him, just to keep things nice?"

Sam laughed. "If you say so. I'm going. Love you again."

"Love you, too. Sleep well, my angel."

She ended the call, her heart lighter than it had been after their last phone call, and laid her head on the pillow. Bob barged back into the room a few seconds later, wrapped in a towel.

She bolted upright with a start and quickly averted her gaze. "Damn, I must have dropped off. And they say women take an eternity in the shower."

"Get out of here… there's a lot of me to wash. You're never satisfied. I'm doing this for your benefit, remember."

"I know. I'm only pulling your leg."

He popped his hairy right leg on his bed and ran his hand up and down it. "And what a beauty it is."

Sam tore off the bed and raced into the bathroom. Before she closed the door, she shouted, "I think my dinner is about to resurface." Then she closed and locked the door behind her, imagining the face he was making. She jumped in the shower herself but made sure she kept her hair dry. It would do for another day. The last thing she needed was to walk around Ennerdale Bridge the following day mimicking a punk rocker.

CHAPTER 7

The village was buzzing the following day. A feeling of pride filled Sam. The locals were out in force from eight, as soon as it got light. The police team had taken the plunge and set off earlier, at seven, hoping to make headway before the others got there. Now it was a waiting game for Sam and the rest of her team. There were the final house-to-house enquiries to conduct at the properties lying on the outskirts of the village. That would keep them busy up until lunchtime, when Rachel was due to arrive.

So far, their enquiries had attained very little in the way of facts. Most of the locals kept to themselves until something like this landed on their doorsteps, then they went all out to join forces.

It was approaching twelve when Sabrina rang Sam to inform her Rachel had shown up. Sam rushed to meet Anita's mother at the Fox and Hounds. She found the two women sitting by the fire in the bar, drinking coffee.

"Ah, here's Sam now, Rachel," Sabrina said.

She went to stand, but Sam motioned for her to remain seated.

"Pleased to meet you, Rachel. Thank you for coming all this way. There's been no news so far today. I contacted the teams as soon as I heard you had arrived."

"I'm devastated that my daughter has gone missing. She loves this area, is always enthralling us with her tales about the walks she's taken around here. This is my first visit to Ennerdale Bridge, and I can see why it means so much to her to be here. I know you said there's been no news this morning, but can you share anything you've gathered since yesterday?"

"Sadly not. Both teams are out there. As the search began earlier than yesterday, I think they'll be fortunate enough to cover more ground. I know a couple of team members have drones at their disposal. We need to think positively that they'll find her today."

"I hope so," Sabrina said.

"Has she taken extra food and water with her?" Sam asked.

"Yes, she is always stocked up, prepared for every eventuality. She should have more than enough supplies to keep her going for a few days. It's whether she has enough clothing with her that is causing doubts in my mind."

Sam placed a hand over Sabrina's. "Luckily, the temperature hasn't really dropped down much at night. We've been fortunate there, or she has."

"But it's still been damp and miserable, that will hamper her, won't it?" Rachel asked.

"If she's an experienced walker then she'll have the nous to hunker down and rest when she can, in order to battle the elements. I'm sure we'll find her soon."

"I hope so. I lost her father a few years ago, and she's all the family I have left."

Sam nodded. "Sorry to hear that. I take it you're close."

"Extremely. There was talk of us moving in together, me

119

in an annex, you know the type of thing. I'm not getting any younger, and she's had her eye on relocating to this area for a while. We had a discussion last week. I told her I was willing to sell up and move with her. That would give her the funds to be able to afford a decent property up here."

Sabrina clutched Rachel's hand. "I didn't know that. I bet she jumped at the chance, didn't she?"

"Yes, we're both excited. She was going to do some walking and then start house-hunting towards the end of her stay. I'm surprised she didn't mention it to you, but then, you know how dedicated she is to her walking, nothing interferes with that, if she can help it."

"That's true. I'd love it if she moved up here. You'll have to be prepared for a constant stream of visitors descending upon you."

Rachel smiled. "You know Anita as well as I do, she'd love the house to be filled with friends. Let's hope the kind people out there, going all out to search for her, find her soon."

"I'm sure that will be the case," Sam said. She rose to her feet and added, "I need to crack on now. It was nice meeting you. We've set up a hub in the Community Room above The Gather. Feel free to pop in and see us if you have any questions. Claire, a valuable member of my team, will be based there during the day, and I'll be popping in and out when I can. We've almost finished with the house-to-house enquiries on another investigation. Don't worry, we're dealing with both cases at the same time, not favouring either of them at present."

"Thank you. We're grateful to you and your teams for the effort you've put in so far."

"We're hoping to have some good news to share with you both soon. In the meantime, all we ask is that you remain positive."

"We will. Thank you, Sam. I feel my daughter's well-being is in safe hands."

"The safest in the area, I can assure you. It's not every day my team and I remain on site for days on end, away from our families, but needs must at a time like this."

"I didn't realise you had put yourselves out for us so much. We're very grateful to you."

"There's no need. We're only doing our jobs at the end of the day, albeit a few miles out of our usual area. I must fly. I'll see you around, ladies."

Sam headed up the road to The Gather. A Land Rover drove past her at speed and screeched to a halt on the road outside the café. Sam's gut went into a spasm, and she upped her pace. By the time she reached the car park she was in a full sprint. "What's going on?" she asked, the instant she set foot inside the café.

"We've had news. They've found her... she's dead!" the man in his sixties said, tears bulging.

Sam had to steady herself on the doorframe as her legs wobbled slightly. Inhaling a large breath, she pulled herself upright and shifted back into professional mode. "Where was she?"

The man turned her way, his face ashen with shock. He moistened his lips with his tongue. "The drone located her. We didn't want to announce it, not until someone reached her to verify that she was dead."

"That makes sense. Are you in touch with the team now?"

"Yes, via my mobile. Do you want to speak with someone out there?"

"Please, I need to ensure they don't go near the body. Is it easy to gain access to it?"

"She was off the track. I don't know how to say this..."

"Just say it. What's going on?"

"She was murdered. At least that's what I think. She didn't die of natural causes, let's put it that way."

"Bugger. I'm going to need you to keep that to yourself for now. Her mother has just arrived in the village, I don't want her freaking out by the news."

"I understand. What a shock this is for those of us who live here, two murders in less than a week."

Sam rubbed the man's upper arm. "I'm sorry you've had to deal with this."

"Hey, don't go feeling sorry for us locals, we were happy to help out, even if the outcome wasn't what any of us expected or wanted."

"What's this?" Emma joined them after coming out of her office.

"They've found Anita, it's not good news. I need to let my team know. Sorry, I didn't catch your name," Sam said to the man who had unknowingly spoilt her day.

"It's Warren Daniels."

"Can you get in touch with the people who are with her now? Remind them not to move the body. We're going to need her exact location for when the pathologist and his team arrive."

"I reckon it will be better if he goes out there via boat. I can ask my mate if we can borrow his, it's no bother."

"That would be fantastic, Warren. I appreciate you going the extra mile for us."

"Nonsense, it's what we do around these parts, isn't it, Emma?"

Emma smiled warmly at Warren. "It is." Then her smile faded. "How awful that she's lost her life. Was it due to the weather, or did she have a fall or something?"

Warren and Sam looked at each other.

"I'll leave you to tell her," Warren said. "I'll make my calls outside, around the back out of earshot of everyone."

"Thanks, Warren." Sam tugged on Emma's arm and led her outside. "Warren thinks she's been murdered. I'd rather not let that snippet of information out of the bag just yet. We should let the pathologist be the one to make that call. Oh God, I need to tell my team and then head back to Anita's mother and Sabrina, to inform them."

"You go. Take a breath now and again, though, Sam, otherwise you're going to burn yourself out, love."

"No chance, not once the adrenaline kicks in. Speak later."

Sam bolted up the stairs two at a time. "Claire, they've found her."

Claire's face lit up until Sam shook her head.

"Damn, she's dead, isn't she?" Claire lashed out at her desk. "Bugger, I was really hoping that we'd find her this morning… alive."

Sam sank into the chair next to Claire. "And what's worse, is their initial findings are indicating that she's been murdered."

"Christ, really? That's not good news, boss."

"Tell me about it. I'll ring Bob, tell him, Liam and Oliver to get back here. Can you contact our search team? I'm waiting on the exact location. Warren, the chap who told me, is arranging the transportation to the scene, via boat. He reckons it'll be easier for the pathologist and his team to access the body from there."

"Gosh, I suppose that would make sense." Claire picked up her phone to make the call.

Sam fished out her mobile and rang her partner. "It's me. They've found her."

"Thank fuck for that. Where?"

"Don't get your hopes up, they found *her body*. Looks like we've got another murder on our hands, Bob."

"Shit! Do you want us to come back? We've almost finished here."

"How many houses are left?"

"Two or three at the most."

"You might as well complete the job, that'll be one less thing to deal with in the coming days. I'm going to head back to the pub and break the news to her mother and Sabrina."

"I think we've got the better end of the deal."

"You sure have. Claire's contacting the search team now."

"See you soon, and Sam?"

"Yes, Bob."

"So sorry it has come to this. I had high hopes that we were going to find her. I suppose the longer the search went on the less confident I became but…"

"I know, it's a bummer nevertheless. We did our best. See you later."

Sam ended the call and sucked in a long breath which she released slowly. It did the trick of slowing down her racing heart rate. "Damn, I'd better get back to the pub."

Claire gave her a weary smile. "I feel for you, boss. Hope it goes well… umm… forget I said that. Stupid bloody thing to say in the circumstances."

Sam smiled. "Don't beat yourself up about it, hon. I shouldn't be long." She left the room and forced her legs to work properly on the walk back to the pub.

Sabrina and Rachel were still in the same seats, relaxing by the fire.

Sabrina narrowed her eyes as soon as she laid eyes on Sam but didn't say anything.

"Hello again, Sam. Any news for us?" Rachel asked. She had a bit more colour in her cheeks now, after sitting next to the fire for so long.

Sam sat in the chair next to Rachel and covered her hand with hers. "I'm sorry, I've just heard that they've found Anita. Sadly, she wasn't alive when they discovered her."

Rachel withdrew her hand and covered her face, and Sabrina just seemed shellshocked by the news.

"I'm so sorry," Sam said. "I can't tell you more than that at the moment, not until the pathologist gives me his assessment once he's carried out a thorough examination." *Damn, I should have bloody rung him.* Sam removed her phone from her pocket and dropped Claire a text, asking her to make the call. *What is the matter with me? My head is all over the place today.*

Rachel sobbed and sobbed. Sam respected her grief and didn't say anything for a few minutes. Sabrina did her best to comfort Rachel, but she pulled away from her touch. Eventually, Rachel's hands dropped into her lap. Sabrina gave her a tissue, and she blew her nose.

"I'm sorry, I don't know what came over me… I suppose you never know how you're going to react to the news that your child is… gone. Damn, after losing her father, too. How cruel can this life be when you least expect it? You have to tell me; how did she die?"

It was the one question Sam feared Rachel would ask, above all others. "We're not sure yet. The search team located her via a drone they had deployed. We won't be able to fill in the blanks until the pathologist gets to the scene. He's on his way," Sam fibbed.

Rachel shook her head over and over and then reached for Sabrina's hand. "I'm so grateful to you for contacting me, Sabrina. I would have detested hearing this kind of news over the phone."

"That would never happen," Sam said. "A local officer would have delivered the news in person."

"I didn't know that," Rachel replied. "Not that it matters."

"What happens now?" Sabrina licked her dry lips.

"We're stuck until the pathologist has examined Anita's body. He shouldn't be long. One of the locals is arranging for a boat to take the pathologist to the site, rather than go via the often boggy route."

"That makes sense. The path can be quite rocky, too, and if the team aren't used to trekking, that might put obstacles in the way," Sabrina said. She stared down at her ankle and rotated it, as if it were giving her trouble.

"Is it okay?" Sam asked.

"Yes, it goes to sleep now and again."

"Maybe you should get it checked out at the hospital, in that case."

"I'll be fine. We have more important things to worry about than my blasted ankle."

Rachel shook her head. "You should listen to the inspector. You might cause further damage by not getting it checked out. I could take you. It would distract us for a while, allowing the pathologist to get here and assess the situation."

Sam resumed practicality mode with Rachel. Anything and everything should and would be tackled, rather than her daughter's death becoming centre stage. She'd witnessed this kind of behaviour so many times over the years when she'd needed to break the sad news of a loved one passing, especially that of an older child. Her heart went out to the woman, who was doing her very best to deal with her daughter's death in a dignified fashion, one that Sam very much admired.

"I can arrange for an officer to take you; the hospital is only about ten minutes up the road."

Sabrina shook her head. "Honestly, I'm fine. I can get my ankle sorted later. I'd much rather stick around here, feel close to Anita. Sorry if that sounds silly, now that she's been found. I can't believe she's gone. I never expected this to be the outcome. I should have made her bring me back to the village instead of persuading her to go on without me. I thought I was doing the right thing for both of us at the time."

Sam wagged a finger. "No, you really mustn't do that, Sabrina. Blaming yourself isn't going to bring Anita back. I'm sure Rachel will agree."

"Wholeheartedly. Don't do it, Sabrina. We both know how determined Anita could be at times. I shall miss her terribly. She's been my absolute rock since her father's passing, and now..." Rachel broke down again.

Sam glanced sideways when the door of the pub opened and in walked Gertrude.

She approached them with concern etched into her features. "Sorry to intrude. Is everything all right, Sam?"

Sam stood and invited Gertrude to join her at another table. "Sadly, the missing lady, Anita, has been found. She's dead."

Gertrude sank onto the stool and stared at Sam, and then her gaze slowly turned towards Sabrina and Rachel. "Oh no, how terrible." Her voice lowered, and she asked, "Did she die of natural causes?"

"I can't say, not at this time, not until the pathologist has shared his thoughts, and that won't be for at least an hour or two."

"But do you suspect foul play? Surely you can tell me that after what's happened to Patricia? Two deaths within a few days in such an idyllic area... you don't have to be a genius to join the dots, do you?"

Sam quickly glanced at Rachel and Sabrina, ensuring their conversation hadn't been overheard. "I can't say any more than I have already, Gertrude."

"I'm saying it for you," Gertrude insisted. "Wake up, Inspector. You have a killer walking amongst us, and you and

127

your team need to find them... quickly." Her tone had become sharper, and her voice was now strained with emotion.

Rachel turned to ask, "What's going on? Is there something I should know?"

Sam swallowed down the acid burning her throat. "No, this is Gertrude Nunez, a friend of the lady whose body was discovered in the forest the other day."

"Oh, I see. Well, if you have something to say, I think we should all hear it."

Gertrude nodded. "I think the inspector is guilty of keeping something very important from you."

"Don't do this, Gertrude," Sam warned. "I've done no such thing."

"Don't stop the lady from talking. I'm listening," Rachel said.

"Think about it. My girlfriend was murdered in this village, and now your daughter has died. Ask yourself this, why? Was she healthy?"

Rachel nodded.

"How does a healthy person keel over and die? No, I believe the inspector knows far more than she's letting on. She needs to be frank and honest with you, in my opinion, otherwise she's going to lose all credibility."

"It's not as simple as that, Gertrude. My hands are genuinely tied until the pathologist arrives and gives his professional assessment."

"Is she right? Is there something more sinister about my daughter's death that you're not telling me?" Rachel demanded.

"I'm not trying to deceive you, I swear. We have procedures we need to follow."

Rachel stood and approached Sam. "I don't care about those. Did my daughter, a very healthy young lady when she set off from Bristol a few days ago, I hasten to add, die of natural causes or not?"

Feeling intimidated all of a sudden, Sam rose to her feet. "I'm telling you this news against my better judgement."

"Don't stop there. I have a right to know, don't I?"

Sam sighed. "It's not about rights at this stage in the proceedings, it's about getting the facts straight. If I tell you one thing and it turns out to be totally false, what will you think of me then? Furthermore, I prefer not to reveal what I've been told until I have witnessed the results for myself."

"By that, I take it my daughter didn't die of natural causes and something far more disturbing is afoot here, is that the case, Inspector? Tell me, damn you!" she shouted impatiently.

Sam closed her eyes and let out a sigh. "Again, I prefer to deal in facts and not gossip, so forgive me if I choose to keep the information from you for now."

Rachel took a step closer and prodded Sam in the chest. "I demand to speak with your senior officer."

"If you must, but I'm sure he'll tell you the same."

"We'll see about that."

Sam removed her phone from her pocket and dialled the station. She asked the control room to put her through to DCI Armstrong on an urgent matter.

"DI Cobbs, what's so urgent that you feel the need to interrupt an important meeting I'm having with a cheese sandwich?"

"Sorry to disturb you, sir…"

Before Sam could say anything else, Rachel snatched the phone out of her hand.

"I'm Rachel Davila. I've just been informed by the inspector here that my daughter is dead, and yet she's refusing to tell me how my twenty-nine-year-old daughter, who arrived in this area fit and healthy, has died… Okay, while I appreciate she has to be cautious, am I not entitled to know the facts...? This is ridiculous, I feel the inspector is hiding something from me and I have a right to know how Anita died, don't I...? No, this is shambolic, absolutely despicable behaviour... and who is your senior officer...? Yes, I'll be having a word with him about you covering your inspector's back." Tears dripped onto Rachel's cheeks. "I don't give a damn..." she choked. "I have a right... don't make me beg... Yes, she's here, I'll pass the phone back to her."

"Sir, I tried to tell Mrs Davila that there are certain procedures we need to adhere to in circumstances such as this."

"Sam, listen to me, they're guidelines, that's all. Each situation should be treated on its own merit, you of all people should know that. Give the lady the information she needs, that's an order."

"Yes, sir. Sorry to have disturbed your lunch."

"Think nothing of it. Do the right thing, Sam."

"Yes, sir." Sam ended the call and invited Rachel to take a seat next to her.

They both sat, if a little reluctantly on Rachel's part.

"I've been ordered to tell you everything I know, but I want you to realise this is against my better judgement and I hope there's no comeback on me."

Rachel sighed, and her lip quivered. "There won't be, just get on with it, Inspector."

Sam had come across this type of situation before, a parent being aggressive, although usually it was a male member of the family. "I'm only going to tell you what I've heard. Please don't bombard me with questions I cannot answer."

"Okay."

"I've been told that a drone found your daughter, and when the rescue team arrived it was confirmed that your daughter had died by foul means."

"What? How exactly?"

Sam shrugged. "I can't say more than that, I'm sorry, that truly is as much as I've been told."

"So, both women have been murdered?" Gertrude butted into the conversation.

"Unfortunately, that appears to be the case," Sam admitted. "Now, if you'll excuse me, I have work to do. I've carried out my duty, telling the next of kin, now I have a killer to catch before they target someone else in this beautiful village."

"Of course," Rachel said, her tone a lot calmer. "Don't let us hold you up. I'm sorry it came to this, me seeking the truth by going over your head."

"All I was doing was protecting you until I had the full facts to hand. I apologise for doing that instead of telling you the truth."

"I appreciate your thoughtfulness, Inspector, but I believe a parent has the right to know a significant detail of this magnitude from the outset."

"Ordinarily, I might agree with you, had I seen Anita's body for myself. We're going around in circles here. I will promise to be more open with you going forward, if that's what you want?"

"I do."

"And so do I," Gertrude said.

Sam didn't have it in her to smile at the women, she simply nodded and left the pub. Outside, she bumped into Bob, Liam and Oliver who had just got out of Liam's car. "Boy, am I relieved to see you guys. I could have done with backup a few minutes ago."

Bob frowned. "Has someone been hassling you? You want me to have a word with them?"

"No, there's no need for that. I'll tell you all about it later. We need to get back to the hub and go through what our next step is going to be. Des is on his way, or he should be by now."

"We could do with a bacon roll, eh, lads?"

Liam and Oliver appeared embarrassed by Bob's question, and Sam merely shook her head.

"I have no words. Come on."

They set off on foot and rounded the corner to The Gather to find a couple of uniformed officers talking to an irate young man.

Sam upped her pace. "Is something wrong?"

"Yes, ma'am. This young man has informed us that his mother has gone missing."

A sinking feeling hit Sam in the solar plexus with full force. "Okay, shall we take this upstairs?"

The young man was frantic, his hands nervously twiddling with the sleeves of his cycling T-shirt. "No, I have to find her. She must be here somewhere. You have to take me seriously. I'm not messing about, Mum was here one minute and gone the next."

"What's your name?" Sam asked.

"Paul Mayer. My mother is called Lisa. Please, you have to help me. If someone has taken her then they're getting away."

"I'm going to need a few more facts before I can put anything in place. How do you know your mother is missing?"

"That's her bike, there." He pointed at a silver-trimmed cycle, slotted into the rack next to them. "I've checked inside the cafe, she's not in there."

"Are you local? Could she have stopped off at one of the houses nearby for a chat with someone?"

"No, we're from Workington, we come here a lot, to cycle the area, but she doesn't know anyone, as such, in the village, only to smile and say hello to if she spots a familiar face from our time at the café. Take my word for it, she's gone. I'm begging you; you need to do something quickly."

"Bob, take Liam and Oliver and these two officers with you. Block the roads in and out of the village."

The five of them tore off down the slight incline to fetch their respective cars.

Sam placed her hand on Paul's arm and led him into the café. "Let's do a final check around here first. Could she be in the toilet?"

"No, I've checked. I'm telling you; I've looked everywhere. Please believe me, she's gone."

"Who has?" Emma came up behind them.

"This young man's mother has just disappeared."

"Oh no, not another one," Emma said under her breath.

Sam ignored the comment and walked further into the café. The tables were all full, as usual, with parties of either four or six.

"Is she here?" Sam asked, already knowing what Paul's response was going to be.

"No, I've told you, why won't you believe me? We're wasting time. After what happened to the other cyclist, you should be all over this. I need your help, please, don't delay things any longer."

Sam smiled at the young man. "I'm not, I've already instructed my team to block the roads, that's all I can do right now. Is she carrying a mobile with her?"

"Damn, why didn't I think of that? Yes, I'll try and call her."

The number rang three times and then went dead.

Paul glanced up, his forehead wrinkled with confusion. "That's strange, she always answers her phone. Why isn't she doing it now?"

"Try to keep calm. Come upstairs with me, and we'll get a few details down."

They weaved their way through the tables, and Paul followed Sam upstairs.

Claire glanced up from her computer screen and frowned. "Everything all right, boss?"

"I'm not sure is the truthful answer, Claire. We found Paul outside. Apparently, his mother seems to be missing."

Claire shared a knowing look with Sam that conveyed the same sentiments as Emma.

"Oh. Obvious question," Claire said, "does your mother have a phone with her? Maybe we can try and trace it."

"Good idea. Yes, Paul tried to call it, but it rang off. The rest of the team are putting up roadblocks on the routes in and out of the village. Hopefully we'll locate her soon."

"May I?" Paul asked, pointing at the chair close to Claire's desk.

"Of course," Sam replied.

"I only nipped to the loo. I was busting after our long trip. Mum told me to go on ahead and she would deal with the bikes. She must have done that because they're both locked up, but what happened next? That's what I want to know. Where is she?"

"Were you in the toilet long?"

"No, a quick in-and-out job. Damn, do you think I should call my father?"

"It might be an idea. Where is he?"

"In Workington. He gave us a lift part of the way today. He had a fundraiser meeting up the road. Mum and I accepted the lift but told Dad that we'd make our own way home."

"Do you want to make the call, or shall I do it for you?"

"I think I should do it. Dad is a bit apprehensive about talking to people over the phone. It's nuts, I know, given his job."

"And that is?"

"He's the head of a charity, or should I say joint head, along with our friend, Barbara." He withdrew his phone again from his bum bag and dialled the number. "Dad, I know you're in a meeting, but this is urgent. Mum's gone missing… I'm telling you; she has. I'm here at Ennerdale Bridge, you know that nice café we always come to when we're in the area. I'm upstairs, speaking with the police… You'll come? That's great, thanks, Dad. Not sure if I can handle this on my own… yes, I called her, but the phone went dead after a few rings. Okay, I'll see you in twenty minutes. Drive carefully." He ended the call. "He's as shocked as I am. There's no reason on this earth why Mum should go off like this."

"Believe me, we're going to do all we can to find her. Try not to worry too much. So, you pulled up, desperate for the toilet. Did you see anyone lingering outside the café when you arrived?" Sam asked. She perched on the table nearest to him.

He paused to think and then shook his head. "No, nothing is registering with me. I guess I was in too much of a rush to relieve myself." He ran a trembling hand through his hair. "Why didn't I take note of my surroundings? Why did I leave her outside? Why? If I'd been more observant this wouldn't have happened."

Sam smiled and leaned forward to pat his forearm. "There's no point in blaming yourself, it's not going to do any good. The café is full to the brim, and there are a few coppers in the vicinity, so thinking logically about it, I would hazard a guess that your mother has just wandered off somewhere and nothing menacing has taken place."

"But where would she go? Why? Our intention was to have a drink here, along with something to eat, a late lunch because we were that keen to get on the road neither of us thought about having anything to eat at home."

135

Sam's phone rang. She held a finger up. "It's my partner. Hold that thought. Bob, what have you got?"

"Nothing, I've rung around the others, and they haven't had anyone trying to get out of the village, either."

"What about the road leading up to the lake, is anyone covering that?"

"Liam is there and, like I said, nothing."

"Okay, it was just a thought, bearing in mind what we discovered this morning."

"Understood. How long do you want to keep the roads closed off?"

"As long as it takes to find her, Bob. I'll be in touch if anything comes to light at this end."

"Roger that. Still in need of that bacon roll... just saying."

Sam ended the call with the jab of a finger. "Nothing at all, yet. Do you have a recent picture of your mother on your phone?"

"Oh, yes, I should have thought about that." He angled his mobile in her direction. "This was taken a few days ago. Mum and Dad celebrated their twentieth wedding anniversary. Her smile lit up every room she walked into."

"I can tell, she's a beautiful woman. Can you send me the photo? I'll distribute it amongst my team members, see if that helps."

His fingers worked their magic. Sam gave him her number, and the photo appeared on her tiny screen moments later. She sent it to the rest of the team who, one by one, sent a thumbs-up.

"Are you sure your mother doesn't know anyone in the area?"

"Not really, no. I mean, yes, I'm sure, but I can't get my head around why she would go off like that when our intention was to have something to eat and drink here. Anyway, she's got enough manners not to disappear like that, without telling me where she's going first. I'm fearing the worst here, Inspector. We heard about that female cyclist losing her life a few days ago. Mum hesitated about coming here today but figured it would be fine, safe with a police presence in the vicinity. How wrong that assumption turned out to be. I'm never going to be able to forgive myself for leaving her the way I did. If anything terrible happens to her... well, it has already, hasn't it? She's been kidnapped."

"Please, we don't know that to be the case, yet. Let's not jump to conclusions and worry ourselves even more." Sam leapt to her feet. "I'll be right back." She rushed down the stairs and went in search of Emma. She found her sitting at her desk, her head buried in her hands in floods of tears. "No, no, no, Emma, what's wrong?"

Emma dropped her hands and faced her. "It's all these people, or should I say women, going missing. I can't help wondering why, what's going on? They're all tourists, no one local, why?"

Sam sat on the desk beside her. "That's what is bugging me. It might just be a coincidence, we've yet to figure out what the motive is behind the murders or the women going missing."

"I feel so inadequate, sitting here, when I should be out there, looking for them."

Sam wagged her finger. "Now you're being blooming ridiculous. You've got a business to run. You're doing more than your fair share for the community, keeping us all going for one thing, what with this being the only café in the area. You and your staff are doing a sterling job, but then you always do, hon."

"Nothing you say will alter how hopeless I'm feeling."

"There's no need for it, love. Stop punishing yourself for something that is out of your control."

"I won't be able to do it. Two women already dead, and

now this woman has gone missing right outside our front door, on my watch if you like. Please, don't tell me how ridiculous I'm being, not when something as devastating as this is happening. Who the bloody hell is doing this, Sam?"

"I wish I knew. We've set up roadblocks at either end of the village, however, the call was probably made too late to have stopped the person getting away."

"What a dreadful situation, one of many that has crossed my path this week, I hasten to add. Isn't there anything else you can do, Sam? Flood the area with yet more police?"

"I can understand why you would ask that, but heck, there were coppers all around, and the woman was still kidnapped, or that's what we're thinking at this stage. I know a lot of our men are still out by the lake, but anyone with a smattering of brain cells would consider that before swooping... and in broad daylight. This person must have some cojones."

Emma gasped. "I've just had a thought, what if the culprit is a woman?"

"You could be right. Your guess is as good as mine. I need to get back to her son. What I came down here to ask is whether you have any cameras installed."

Emma closed her eyes and tutted. "It was the next job on the list after putting the solar panels in. Damn, maybe I should have made it a priority. In my defence, look around you, this is normally a quiet, sleepy community. I really didn't feel it was necessary to have cameras."

"I totally understand your reasoning. It was worth a shot. I hadn't felt the need to ask before. Okay, come on, chin up, love, soldier on, it's what we do, isn't it?"

"I suppose so. Give me a shout if you need me to do anything, like organise another bloody search team."

Sam puffed out her cheeks. "Hopefully, it won't come to

that and we'll find her soon. We're doing all we can at present. The son rang his father, he's on his way."

"Good, I hate the thought of that young man being alone at a time like this."

"He won't be, we'll make sure of it. Stay strong and get these silly thoughts out of your head, you hear me?"

"Yes, Mum."

Sam smiled and pecked her friend on the cheek then swept out of the office.

CHAPTER 8

"*That* was a close one, that copper must have seen me."

More than likely, because you're a prick and never do things properly. Fancy kidnapping the damn woman in broad daylight when there are ruddy police in the area.

"I know, but I was desperate to have her. She was there, begging to be taken." He took a step closer to the unconscious woman lying on the bale of straw. He'd secured her with a large chain he used to restrain the cattle when he needed to inject them with medication against one ailment or another. He stared at her long and hard. She was like her. Very similar build, and her hair colour was pretty much the same. The woman hadn't known what hit her. A swift right hook had knocked her down. He'd swooped and bundled her in the back seat of his car before anyone had either arrived at or departed The Gather.

That place is the perfect hunting ground. We should have considered it sooner. You did well, mate. We both did.

"How long before she wakes up?"

Could be minutes or even hours. I don't think you realise how strong you are, and that right hook was fierce. Muhammad Ali wouldn't have been able to have dodged that one and would have hit the deck with force.

"Get away with you. Shit, could her jaw be damaged? I can't see from this angle. Maybe it's broken."

I think that's a fair assumption. She's been out cold for about an hour now. Go on, give her a poke...

Picking up the metal bar he used to prod his cattle with when he expected them to move on, he tapped her lightly on the knee. The woman didn't respond. So, he prodded again, harder this time, and she stirred a little. Her eyes inched open a touch and then widened when he took a step forward.

"Please, don't hurt me. Why are you doing this to me? I've got money, if that's what this is all about."

"It's not. Shut up. Only speak when I tell you to, and we'll get along just fine. Are you hurt?"

She took a moment to check herself over. "I don't think so, except for my jaw, it's throbbing."

"It might be broken. I'm sorry, I never meant to hurt you, not really. I had to seize the opportunity, you know, strike while the iron was hot, to bring you here."

"And where is *here?*"

He tutted. "I warned you not to speak until you were spoken to, you have no right to ask any questions." He whacked her ankle with the rod.

She screamed, and he ran forward and shoved an oily cloth in her mouth. She gagged.

"What did I tell you? If you're not going to follow the rules, I see very little point in keeping you alive. I'll get rid of you like the others. It didn't take much for them to piss me off, either. Learn by their mistakes, and all will be good, and you'll live to see another day. Do you have any children?"

She nodded.

"How many? Stamp your feet to give me the answer."

She stamped her foot once.

"Was your son the one who left you to fend for yourself today."

She nodded.

"Silly boy, especially when there's a killer on the loose in the village."

Stop talking to her, you're telling her you have feelings doing that. You don't give a shit about her—we don't give a shit, do we?

"No, not really," he muttered his reply.

She inclined her head as if to ask him to repeat what he'd said.

"It doesn't matter, I was talking to myself... I do that a lot."

He noticed the fear seep into her eyes. He got a thrill when that appeared. The control over another human being was the icing on the cake for him. He revelled in it. Grabbed it with both hands once the opportunity arose.

Wondering if she was secured well enough, he tested the ropes binding her ankles and wrists together. Even if they were on the dodgy side, there's no way she would escape the chain around her neck; that was his intention, after all.

"Are you thirsty?"

She nodded again. He fetched a ladle of water from the barrel in the corner. She turned her face away from him.

He tore the rag out of her mouth and ordered, "Drink it. You wanted it, woman."

"I don't know how long it's been there. It might be full of bloody bacteria for all I know."

He shoved the cloth back in her open mouth at the end of her speech, picked up the rod and bashed her other ankle with it. A muffled scream filled the barn, and tears welled up in her eyes.

"Oh no, did I hurt you? That's because you rejected my kindness. Folks like you need to appreciate that there are

142

some people in this world who go out of their way to treat others well."

She simply stared back at him.

"Do you want something to eat?"

She shook her head.

"Suit yourself, you can starve for all I care."

A single tear dripped onto her cheek.

Aww... look at that, she's going for the sympathy vote. Don't fall for it, big man. Let her frigging suffer. She needs to learn who's in charge around here. Us.

"You're right. I need to make sure she eats and drinks, though, wouldn't want her going downhill quickly, would we now?" He laughed, and so did the voices in his head. Despite his lonely existence, out here, in the middle of nowhere, he was never alone, not really. He got up close to his prisoner, and she leaned back into the bale of straw behind her. "Don't worry, I won't hurt you... yet. You need to keep on your toes around me, just warning you. Don't even think about overstepping the mark, it'll only end one way."

She shook her head and remained as stiff as a board until he retreated. Once he reached the door of the barn, he turned to look back at her to find her shoulders now relaxed, even if there was fear resonating in her eyes. He pointed at her. "Remember, do as I say, and you and me are going to get along just fine. If you don't..." He placed his thumb on the right side of his neck and pulled it across to the left. "You've been warned, lady. Tick me off, and it'll be the last thing you do, got that?"

She had the sense to nod.

He secured the barn with the padlock and made his way back to the farmhouse, noting that some of the brickwork had come away from the gable end.

Just what we need, eh? Hey, here's a thought, we could always

143

up our game, kidnap others and hold them to ransom to fund the repairs on this place.

"Or we could get shot of it altogether. It's a money pit now. I'm sinking every penny I've got into it, only to have yet another part of it fall into disrepair. I can't keep up with the maintenance, not at my age."

Nonsense, we're spring chickens compared to some of the other inhabitants. Hey, here's another thought we've neglected to consider up until now.

"What's that?"

Pointing the finger at someone else in the village, to keep the police off our scent.

"Won't doing that turn the tables on us? Won't they think it's suspicious, me speaking out, accusing someone else in the village?"

Yeah, you've got a point, I never thought of that. As you were then. We'll plod on with the plan we've put into action and think nothing more about that dumb idea.

"I'm not saying it was a dumb idea but I do think we need to be a bit cautious. It's a small village, word could spread like wildfire if we let it."

I agree. You need to continue to portray yourself as a helpful individual. That'll put them off the scent, not that they've managed to pick up one as yet. Stupid cops, especially the one in charge, the female. We could wipe the floor with her. Put a large dent in any likely promotions she might be up for in the future. If she can't handle a trivial investigation like this one, there's no hope for her, is there?

"Trivial investigation is a bit far off the mark. They're up shit creek, searching for the murderer of two women. How many times has that happened over the years up here?"

Never. Hey, they'd better get their fingers out or there will be a third victim coming their way soon, unless you go down the ransom route. Just a suggestion.

144

"No, I don't want to stray too far from our plans at this time. We should stay on course and stick to what we know best, for now."

If you say so. I'm starving, what have we got to eat?

Opening the fridge, he groaned. It was empty except for a few blackened carrots, a jar of pickled onions and a block of mouldy cheese. He wandered over to the bread bin and found the remains of half a loaf. "Looks like cheese on toast again. I don't have the funds to go shopping for food, not until my pension drops into the bank. That's due to arrive at the end of the week."

It'll have to do. No mouldy bits, though, I've had my share of them over the years.

"It's supposed to be good for you, in moderation. A vital source of penicillin, so my old gran used to say. Trouble is, everything is so anal with regard to produce going out of date. All this confusion about use-by or sell-by dates. My old gran would be turning in her grave if she had to walk the earth these days. No wonder people's immune systems are shot. I remember thinking nothing about playing in a pool of mud when I was a kid. My gran caught me putting a worm in my mouth when I was a toddler."

Eww... don't even go there. That sounds horrendous. I don't remember those days. Was I around then?

"No, you didn't come on the scene until much later, when times got tough and I started doubting my course, and the values I had left, to make it in this life. Right about the time Mum and Dad passed away. That was a dreadful year, that was. Life began spiralling to a different level then."

Get over it! The oldies died years ago. There's no point dwelling on that now, we have work to do.

"I'm well aware of that. I need to sit down and think about what our next step is going to be, after I've had something to eat." He popped a couple of pieces of bread under the grill and sliced some cheese which he placed on the other side once one side of the bread was toasted, all the time the voice in his head working on ideas, swirling like an out-of-control tornado. In the end, his snack started smoking, leaving him to deal with the burnt offerings.

Holding his head in his hands and spinning around on the spot, he shouted, "Shut up! Leave me alone. I can't handle you now. I need to figure out what to do for the best."

The best thing to do would be to kidnap another, and soon... as in today. Without a doubt, that'll keep the coppers on their toes.

That got him thinking while he placed another couple of pieces of bread under the grill and sliced up the last of the cheese. "How can I kidnap someone else so soon? The coppers will be extra vigilant now, won't they?"

Not necessarily, no. Anyway, we're not likely to know unless we try.

His heart skipped along merrily and then stopped for several seconds, only to start and then skip some more. He held a clenched hand over his chest and thumped it, hoping to get his heartrate back to near normal again. Luckily, the deed worked a treat and everything was fine once more. He'd shown no signs of distress in that department before. He'd need to be more careful in the future.

CHAPTER 9

*A*n hour or so after Paul's mother went missing, Sam found herself in a total spin.

Bob nudged her and took her to one side without the rest of the team noticing. "Are you okay? You don't look it."

"I'm fine. I hate it when we're being hit from all sides. The body of the second victim is due back from the lake anytime soon, and I've yet to deal with the irate husband of the third suspected victim. His son has taken him downstairs for a coffee to see if that will calm him down before he starts having a go at me again."

"Yeah, that was totally uncalled for, as if his wife going missing was your fault. Some people need to get a life."

"Don't be too hard on him, Bob, I think I would have reacted exactly the same if I had been in his shoes. Look around you at the number of police officers we have on duty in this village. We must be outnumbering the locals by now, and still this shithead swoops in and manages to kidnap someone from under our damn noses."

"We were all busy at the time, dealing with what's happened with the other two victims. We weren't expecting another one to go missing within a few feet of us. Tell me how we're supposed to prevent things like that from occurring, and I'll tell you that, if we could do that, then there would be no need to have a police force, full stop."

Sam shook her head, and her brow pinched into a frown. "Sometimes your thinking defies all logic."

It was Bob's turn to frown. "What's that supposed to mean?"

"About as much as your logic did, so now we're even."

"Whatever. What's next? With no cameras outside the café and no witnesses, what the fuck is left open to us?"

Sam paused to mull over his question.

But, after a few seconds, it was Liam who answered Bob. "We could ask the punters downstairs if anyone has a dashcam that works while their vehicle is immobile."

"What about the neighbour next door? Maybe they'll have a camera up," Oliver suggested.

"Okay, you both do what's necessary to check those angles, and the three of us will put our heads together to see what else we can come up with."

Liam and Oliver marched out of the room, on a mission, leaving Bob, Claire and Sam all pondering the situation, trying to figure out where they were going wrong.

Sam shook her head. "His balls must be made of cast iron."

"Whose?" Bob asked.

"The kidnapper. To abduct someone in a crowded place when the village is overwhelmed by a police presence is totally unthinkable."

"Either that or the fucker has a death wish," Bob mumbled. "Screwed-up effing idiot."

"He or she may be screwed up, but here's the thing, partner, they got away with it. So maybe they're not as screwed up as we've been assuming they are."

"What are you saying? That you're admiring their skills? I've frigging heard it all now."

"Don't be so ridiculous, that's not what I'm implying at all. What I'm trying to do is point out the obvious."

"Except you're not. The lad said there were no police here, outside the café when he and his mother pulled up. So that kind of dismisses your theory, doesn't it?"

"Okay, maybe you're right. But I was a matter of a few feet away at the pub, dealing with the other victims' families. The kidnapper, or killer, must have been aware of that."

"So, what are you suggesting now? He or she is enjoying the game? Playing with us, treating us like prize morons? Taking pleasure teaching us a lesson in front of the whole village?"

"All of the above. We won't know for sure until we find the culprit and question them."

"Whatever. I know one thing, going round and round in circles up here isn't going to help us find that poor woman."

Sam crossed her arms tightly and tapped her foot. "Okay, smartarse, pray tell me where you think I'm going wrong."

Bob shuffled his feet. Sam knew he'd realised he'd overstepped the mark, querying the position they were in.

"I'm sorry, for speaking out of turn."

"Apology accepted. You know as well as I do that we're doing our very best here, partner. We're up against a wicked person, intent on causing havoc within a close-knit community. The question is, why? Until we know that, I fear there's going to be very little we can do to prevent the bastard, or bitch, from striking a fourth or fifth time, no matter how galling that is to hear."

"Too right. What do you intend to do, then? Flood the village with yet more cops? I can't see that going down well with either the locals or the boss back at the station, if the

149

outcome is going to be the same, this fucker pouncing and taking someone else right from under our noses."

"I have no intention of allowing that to happen again."

Bob shrugged. "How are you going to stop it? Sorry, I hate sounding negative all the time, but I'm looking from an outsider's point of view at what we've achieved so far, and it ain't looking great."

Sam heaved out a breath. "You're right. Hey, I'm open to any, and all, suggestions. Claire, can you offer any insight into our dilemma?"

The sergeant shook her head. "I'm trying to come up with something, boss, but this whole damn investigation has me flummoxed. Like you say, apart from flooding the village with every officer we have at our disposal, there's very little else we can do, not really. To me, it sounds like the killer or kidnapper, assuming they're the same person, is a risk taker. Enjoying the game of cat and mouse with the police."

"In other words, they're laughing at us."

Claire and Bob both nodded.

"I fear that's what it amounts to, yes," Bob agreed.

Sam kicked out at the nearest chair and sent it scurrying across the room.

"If that's how you're going to treat the furniture…" Emma appeared in the doorway.

Sam's cheeks warmed up under her friend's angry glare. "Sorry, it's the frustration talking."

Emma entered the room and sat at one of the tables. "I'm only winding you up. I couldn't do your job, Sam. I'd definitely have clumps of hair missing at the end of every shift. In fact, I'd more than likely be bald within a week."

Sam laughed. Emma always used to have the ability to make her laugh when things were going against them at school. "Sorry, the image going through my mind is… well, you don't want to know. You used to be so proud of your locks at school, if I recall correctly."

"I still am, can't you tell?" Emma said, her expression deadpan until Sam spotted the glint in her eye.

"Ever the clown. What can we do for you?"

"Nothing, I'm sitting in my office, on edge. It's not doing me any good. I'm overloaded with staff today, so there's nothing for me to do in the café itself. So, I thought I'd come up here and offer to lend a hand."

"Blimey, I don't think anyone has ever offered to lend us a hand before on a murder case, have they, Bob?"

He shrugged. "If they have, I can't remember."

Sam faced her friend and said, "Let's take a walk around the village. I could do with some fresh air, I'm going stir-crazy up here."

"You're on. Let me get my jacket, the breeze has got up out there."

"I'll meet you outside the café in five minutes."

Emma left, and Sam, Claire and Bob took up where they'd left off, except they hadn't got very far in the first place.

"It's so infuriating," Sam said. She aimed a fist at the fleshy part of her thigh.

"Beating yourself up about it ain't gonna help," Bob said.

Footsteps sounded on the stairs outside, and Liam and Oliver both appeared in the doorway.

"Nothing with the punters nor the neighbour next door, boss," Liam told her.

"Damn. We're up the creek without a paddle, now. We could do with a break, and I fear one isn't going to cross our path anytime soon."

"One question that is tapping away at my head," Bob said.

"What's that? Don't keep us in suspense, Bob."

"Do you think we're looking at a local now?"

Sam contemplated his question for a while and then hitched up a shoulder. "Your guess is as good as mine. Maybe it's a tourist, intent on making us think we're dealing with a local."

Bob chewed his lip. "I'd agree with you, except would a tourist know the area well enough to dispose of the first two victims in out-of-reach places, if you get my drift?"

"Hardly out of reach, but yes, I understand where you're going with this. A 'normal killer' per se, if you can label someone with that tag, wouldn't care about trying to hide the body, they would generally leave them in situ. The first victim's body was found in the forest, possibly relocated there, we've yet to have that confirmed, and the second victim was found in the undergrowth, off the usual footpath."

"That's my point, would a tourist have the mindset to consider where they left the bodies?"

Sam winked at her partner. "You might be on to something… however, you and the boys have conducted a house-to-house enquiry throughout the village and come up with a big fat blank."

Bob's feet shifted.

"I'm not dissing your efforts, not in the slightest. All I'm saying is that maybe we should go back over that process, figure out if there were any houses which you might have missed or where you didn't get to speak with the homeowner."

Bob nodded thoughtfully. "We could sit down and go over the details. Are you up for that, Liam and Oliver? Three heads should ultimately be better than one in this instance."

Liam and Oliver both nodded, and the three of them each pulled out a chair around one of the tables.

"I'll be back shortly," Sam said. "I could do with a break."

Sam met up with Emma at the bottom of the stairs. They walked into the village, past the Fox and Hounds and the church, winding their way through the narrow road that led up to the primary school. The children were out, playing on the equipment.

"The innocence of kids, eh? They have no idea what's going on around them most of the time," Emma said. "Who would have thought that Ennerdale Bridge would become like Midsomer?" She shuddered.

Sam flung an arm around her shoulders. "This is a blip, that's all. We'll find the culprit, don't worry. We just need this person to slip up and we'll nail their arses to the fence."

Emma smiled. "Anyone ever tell you that you have a way with words?"

"Quite a few. You knew what I meant, though, didn't you? I don't want you or the locals freaking out about this."

"I think you'll find it's too late for that, Sam. I haven't been off the phone today. Once the locals get a notion into their heads, it festers and festers until... you get the idea."

"I do. We'll figure this out, I promise. We just need one tiny clue to get us up and running. Between you and me, we've come back to the conclusion that we're possibly looking at a local being responsible."

Emma stopped, and her mouth dropped open.

"Don't look like that, it's something that needs to be considered. It's not like we have a choice."

"I suppose you're right. I haven't really wanted to think about that side of things. I put it down to a tourist coming into the area. Oh my, if word gets out, the locals are going to play up something chronic."

"Let's keep it to ourselves for now. Come on, let's have a wander, I'll need to get back to the hub soon."

Emma tilted her head. "What's that noise? It seems to be coming from one of the bushes behind us."

Sam opened the gate to the small cottage they were standing in front of and was immediately told off by the owner of the property, banging on the window at her. Sam produced her ID and showed it to the irate woman. "Sorry, I'm the police. I won't be a moment."

The wizened old lady threw open her window and shouted, "I don't care if you're the Queen of England, God rest her soul. You've got no right trespassing in my garden, walking all over my flowers."

Sam glanced around her feet and noticed the number of weeds choking the flowers in the bed. She didn't have the inclination to argue with her. "I'm sorry, this is police business, it could be vital to our enquiries."

"Go on then. I suppose you could do with all the help you can get. You lot have been hopeless so far."

Charming, thanks for that. We're doing our best with our backs against the wall.

Sam ignored the woman and got down on her haunches to find the source of the noise. It wasn't until she got a few feet away that she realised it was a mobile phone ringing. Trying to keep her balance, she slipped her hand into a latex glove and then reached into the thorny hedge to root around. Finally, she found the phone which she placed in an evidence bag. "Thanks for all your valuable help," she said sarcastically as she left the woman's garden. "We need to get back to the café. I have a suspicion this might belong to Lisa Mayer. I need her family to corroborate it."

"Gosh, I hope you're right."

They raced back to the café, and Sam sought out the family of the missing woman. Standing next to her husband and son, she held the phone up. "Does this belong to Lisa?"

Her husband nodded. "Yes, where did you find it?"

"Down the road, behind a bush. The kidnapper must have thrown it out of their car when they sped away."

"But that means you can follow the route the kidnapper took, doesn't it?"

154

"Possibly. Although the bush was in the middle of the village, down by the bridge, and there are a few possible routes open to the culprit from there. I'll get my men on to it. How are you holding up?"

"Good question," Richard Mayer said. "We're coping, aren't we, Paul?"

His son sighed. "I'm battling the guilt right now."

Sam held up a finger and wagged it. "Stop it, Paul, don't even go there. You went to the toilet, and your mother was taken in broad daylight. There is nothing for you to feel guilty about."

"You can tell me that a million, gazillion times, Inspector, it's never going to stop me feeling that I've let her down."

"Mr Mayer, you need to have a chat with your son."

"Believe me, I've tried. He'll realise it wasn't down to him, once we find her. When is that likely to be?" Richard asked.

Sam had hoped that Claire would come up trumps tracking the woman's phone. The likelihood of that happening now was zilch. "I can't say. I assure you, we're doing all we can to find her."

"Let's hope you're not too late," Richard muttered, to his son's dismay.

"Dad, don't even think that. It's imperative we remain positive, otherwise we might as well pack up our bikes and leave right now."

"Sorry, son, all I was trying to do was be realistic. Two other women have been reported missing this week and… well, they've both been found dead."

Sam felt any response she voiced to that comment would be futile. "I believe we'll find your wife, your mother, soon. Please, don't lose hope." Sam wanted to add more, but judging by the expressions on both their faces it would have been pointless. "I'll get back upstairs to organise my team."

155

"To do what? Hunt for a killer who has abducted my wife?"

"We're doing that right now, sir. It's too early to give up on us. Please, have faith in our abilities."

"If you say so," Richard said. He twisted in his seat to face the opposite direction.

Sam left the café and bumped into Emma outside.

"Gave up on these years ago." Emma took a long drag on a cigarette.

"Bless you. Don't start again, it's not worth all the hassle of trying to get off them again."

Emma threw the cigarette on the ground, stubbed it out with the toe of her shoe, and then picked up the stub which she disposed of in the nearest bin. "Keep Ennerdale Bridge tidy, eh?"

Sam laughed. "You're a card. I have to fly. Oh, and just to let you know, the phone does belong to Lisa Mayer."

"I'm not sure how I feel about that news."

"Feel hopeful, I am. At least we know which direction the kidnapper went in, now."

Emma shrugged. "What if he stopped, threw the phone out of the car and went in the opposite direction?"

"It's a possibility, of course it is. However, I should imagine he or she would be in a blind panic to get out of the village, or away from The Gather, where they abducted Lisa, knowing how busy your café is most of the time. There's one thing in our favour. I spotted a few fingerprints on the phone. Hopefully one of them will belong to the culprit."

"That is good news, and you'll be able to run it through the system and see who it belongs to, right?"

Sam cringed. "Supposedly, but it'll only be beneficial if the culprit already has a police record."

"Shit, I had no idea it worked that way, it's never even

crossed my mind before. You really do have your backs against the wall, don't you?"

"Don't worry, if it's meant to be, we'll work our way around it and come up with the goods, fingers crossed."

"Now that's something I'm capable of doing, keeping everything crossed for you. Will you give me a shout if you need anything else?"

"You have my word. Umm… another round of coffees wouldn't go amiss."

"Go on, I'll see to it now and bring them up myself."

"You're an angel." Sam joined the rest of the team and filled them in on what she'd learned so far regarding the phone which she had put in an evidence bag and sent to the lab. "I know it's not much, but if there's a chance the culprit has been slack and left their fingerprints on the mobile then we've got them bang to rights when we locate them."

"Joy of joys, all we need now is to find the bugger in order for us to match their prints," Bob said, his chin resting on his chest.

"Sod off, Bob. It is what it is, and it's all we have in our favour so far, so don't knock it. I don't know about you guys, but I'm willing to give up my weekend if it comes to that and work through. I can't see us catching this person otherwise, and it wouldn't feel right going home, leading a normal life, knowing that the killer is still out there, for all we know, ready to pounce as soon as our backs are turned. What do you say?"

Bob sighed and shrugged. "The missus ain't gonna be happy, but that's nothing new. What about you, Liam?"

"Works the same for me. Sarah will be knee-deep in wedding invitations and dress patterns. She's aware how important my role as a copper is and knows I'll give up my spare time if I need to. She'll be fine."

Sam narrowed her eyes and laughed. "Are you sure, Liam?

157

Maybe you should run it past Sarah first, before you agree to anything."

"Oliver?" Bob asked.

"Work always comes first with me, and I'm, how shall I put it, oh yes, between girlfriends at the moment."

"Claire?" Sam asked.

"It's fine by me. Mum can look after the kids; she loves having them on a Saturday and Sunday. She spoils them rotten, and Scott is away on a golfing weekend, so no big deal for me either. He'd want me to give it my all to find a serial killer, if that's what we're talking about here."

"Well, one more murder, and yes, this person will absolutely go down in history as a serial killer, more's the pity. Thanks, guys, I knew you wouldn't let me down, you never have in the past. Crap, now all I have to do is break the news to Rhys. Anyone fancy volunteering to do the job for me?"

The men all averted their gazes, and Claire raised a tentative hand. "I'll do it for you, if that's what you really want, boss?"

"I'm glad to see someone has my back around here, Claire." Sam winked at her.

"What? Are you kidding me?" Bob spluttered.

"Joking. Why are you always the one who takes the bait and treats everything I say so seriously?"

"You really expect me to answer that?" Bob blustered. "What about Alex and Suzanna back at the station? Will they be needed to hold the fort there?"

"I'll have a word, they might as well take the weekend off, it's not like they're snowed under with work, none of us are at present. I'm going to allow them to have their usual time off. If things hot up over the next forty-eight hours, we're going to need to call on them. This way they'll be fresh and ready for action."

"It's your call," Bob said. "Do you want us to ring home now?"

"Why not, it's not as if we can do anything else, is it?"

"I think I've already raised that point once."

Sam decided to call Rhys outside. "Hi, are you free to talk?"

"Hey, of course. I'm on my way home, I had a free afternoon, so I thought I'd take the dogs somewhere nice for a long walk. Can you join us? Is that why you're calling because you've caught the culprit and you're on your way home?"

"I wish. No, quite the opposite, I'm afraid."

"What's that supposed to mean?"

Sam closed her eyes and sighed. "Someone else has gone missing. If we don't catch whoever did this by Friday night, I'm going to have to give up my weekend. My team and I are determined to find her. We'll only be able to do that if we stay on site. I'm sorry, darling."

"Don't be. I'd think it strange if you didn't give your all to the investigation, Sam. You're the utter professional, and I've never known you to let a family down who were searching for justice."

"Thanks, Rhys. I try not to where at all possible. I'll give you a ring later, if I get the chance."

"Don't work too hard. That seems a silly thing to say, in the circumstances."

"I won't. Hopefully the culprit will slip up soon and I'll be home before you know it."

"Dream on. Aren't you always telling me that the villains are getting craftier than ever?"

"Yeah, but don't say that too loud."

They both laughed. It felt good to ease the tension knotting her shoulders, even if it was only for a couple of minutes.

"How was work today?"

"Boring, not much fun. Two clients were no-shows. When I rang them, they both said they forgot they had appointments with me."

"Bugger. Can you still charge them?"

"It's not as simple as that, I wish it was. I'm just pulling up outside the house now. Doreen is standing at the window with Sonny up on his hind legs. Both dogs are missing you like crazy."

"I miss all of you as well. Heck, now you've started me off, something has just flown in my eye. I'm going to have to go now, we're up against it. I really want to find this woman before she turns into victim number three."

"Don't let me hold you up. Sending love and best wishes. Hope to see you home shortly."

"That's my biggest wish, too. Take care and enjoy your walk with the dogs. Love you. Oh, and say hello and thanks to Doreen for me."

"I'll be sure to tell her. She looks a little lost without you being here to brighten her day."

"I'll bring her back a jar of local honey from the shop."

"Sounds delicious. Can you stretch to another one?"

"I might. Thanks for being so understanding, Rhys. I shouldn't say this in case I end up with egg on my face, but I feel sure it's only a matter of time before we catch the perpetrator."

"Let's hope so. Good luck. Love you back. And sending kisses and licks from the terrible twosome."

"Gratefully received, see you soon." Sam ended the call, tears misting her eyes. She took a moment to take in the picturesque view and then returned to the hub. "All sorted for me. What about you guys?"

"Yep, done and dusted, left Abigail seething on the phone. She'll get over it," Bob said.

"Sarah was fine. If anything, she sounded relieved and then ran off a list of things she had to either chase up or sort out over the next few days. Which made me glad I'll be otherwise engaged."

Sam smiled.

"Sounds like you've been saved from a fate worse than death," Oliver teased his partner.

"She's fine, most of the time. It's something about planning a wedding that seems to bring out the worst in women. Dad warned me that would happen, he went through the same thing with my mother, many moons ago."

"Being single suits me down to the ground. I can't see that changing anytime soon either, thankfully." Oliver grinned.

Sam thumbed in his direction and shook her head. "Famous last words, eh? We'll remind him of that little speech when Miss Right walks into his life, won't we?"

"Too bloody right we will," Bob agreed.

"Okay, enough fooling around," Sam said, putting an end to the frivolity. "We have three cases we're desperate to solve. Let's do some brainstorming, see if we've missed anything obvious over the last few days. I'm getting the sinking feeling we have."

NOT LONG AFTER, Sam received a call from Des Markham, requesting that she meet him at the car park up at the lake. Bob joined her and insisted he should drive. The journey only took them five minutes. They drove down the same road where Sam had found Lisa's phone which made her eager to keep her eyes peeled.

"The killer might live out this way or be using a property out here, so we need to remain vigilant."

"No change there, that's my usual state."

"I believe you. Houses are few and far between out this

way, compared to the village, so anything's possible. You and the boys did come out this far, didn't you?"

"The boys covered this area. You know how thorough they are; don't you go casting aspersions that are unwarranted."

Sam slapped a hand over her chest. "Me? You've got a bloody cheek."

Bob chortled. "It really doesn't take much to get you going lately."

"Do you know why that is, Bob?"

He shook his head.

"Because I'm so damned focussed on the investigation, nothing else matters. I'm sure Rhys will back me up on that one."

"Oops, okay, there's no need to snap my head off. Are you and Rhys all right? Is there something I should know?"

"We're fine. Stop nit-picking everything I say, reading into things that just aren't there. Besides, if I seem a little more distracted than normal, I think I'm entitled to feel that way after saying farewell to my mother, except I haven't, not yet, the funeral is next week, and I've barely given it a second thought because of this investigation."

"I've told you before, you should have taken time off. It's not like you're not allowed to take compassionate leave. Sometimes, just sometimes, you can be far too hard on yourself, Sam. I'm sorely tempted to give you a kick up the jacksy now and again; however, I have to stop myself, only because I value my job and would miss working alongside you."

"Ditto. I shouldn't have mentioned the funeral. I'm trying to block it out of my mind in case my feelings spiral out of control."

"You know what? Even if they did, no one would think badly of you. You've lost your mother, the person who gave you life, for fuck's sake. That's a massive deal in my opinion."

Sam stared at the road ahead as they took the turning up to the lake, through the wooded area on either side of them.

"Have I upset you?" Bob whispered a few seconds later.

She rested a hand on his thigh. "Not at all. Mum and I… well, I haven't really told you this before, but now and again, granted not all the time, we had what I would describe as a fractious relationship."

"Ah, that explains a lot. Saying that, you still loved her, though, didn't you?"

"Of course I did. It's hard to put into words what I really felt about her. I suppose I'm holding back because I don't want to come across as a hypocrite and be criticised for that. When Crystal said she was willing to deal with the funeral, my relief was palpable."

"Sam, no one is going to judge you, you're being foolish if that's what you believe. Most people favour one parent over the other, without even realising it. I bet you are closer to your father, and Crystal to your mum. I'm right, aren't I?"

Sam faced him and nodded. "You are. I don't care what other people say about you, Bob, you can be a perceptive git when the mood takes you."

He winked at her. "I know. I hide my talent well."

Bob brought the car to a halt close to the pathologist's van. Des was at the rear of the vehicle, stripping off his protective suit, which he shoved into a black bag.

"You took your time," Des teased.

"Don't, I'm not in the mood. I take it you managed to recover the body all right?"

"Yes, hey, you're lucky I didn't get seasick on that blasted boat you provided."

Sam rolled her eyes. "Always one for exaggerating, aren't you? Can you even get seasick on a lake that is as still as a millpond?"

163

"*I can*, I assure you. Anyway, we recovered her, and she's now on the way to the mortuary."

"And?"

"And, there I will carry out the post-mortem on her, as usual. It's not something we're allowed to do out in the field."

"Are you deliberately being obtuse?"

A twinkle materialised in Des's eyes. "I might be testing your will to live, it's a habit of mine."

"No shit, Sherlock. I kind of figured that out for myself. Are you going to divulge what the cause of death was?"

"Strangulation. No sexual intercourse, in case that was going to be your second question."

"It was. Add mind reader to your many talents. So, the killer strangled her and dumped her in the undergrowth."

Des raised an eyebrow. "So it would seem. Are you after my job, Inspector?"

Sam ignored Des's usual impudence as her thoughts raced. "And her body was located a long way into the walk, at least a couple of miles around the lake, but off the track?"

"That's right. What are you getting at?"

Sam shrugged. "We've bounced a few ideas around between us and we've decided that one of the locals is probably responsible for the crimes. How far off the track was she? And what was the terrain like?"

"I'd say around fifteen to twenty feet, maybe twenty-five at a stretch. The terrain was patchy, boggy in parts and rocky in others."

Sam held her chin between her thumb and finger. "The sort of terrain a local would be used to, someone who travelled the route frequently."

"Hard to say. Had she been found a long way off the track, I'd be inclined to agree with you, but she wasn't."

"Hmm... okay, it was just a thought. I need to make you aware that a third woman has gone missing."

"Jesus, in the actual village or in the surrounding area, on the fell itself, or around the lake again?"

"This one was kidnapped under our bloody noses." Sam instantly raised a hand when his mouth opened. "This is no time to fling any criticism or accusations at us."

"Heck, give me a break, as if I would do such a thing!"

"You would," Sam muttered. "We're in the ultimate race against time to find her. I found her mobile dumped behind a bush back in the village. I'm presuming the killer picked the woman up in his car and threw the phone out of the window. We've narrowed it down, we think, to the culprit living out this way."

"Sounds plausible. I noticed a few farms or large houses situated around the lake on the trip out to the crime scene. Might be worth checking them out if you haven't had the chance already."

"Thanks, we'll get on to it right away. Can you send the PM results to me ASAP?"

"As soon as I'm able to, but we both know how likely that's going to be if you keep sending bodies my way. So, you need to up your game, Inspector, and do all you can to prevent anyone else from losing their life."

"It's as easy as that, isn't it? Except it isn't, if we're chasing a killer who knows the area inside out, better than we do." Sam stepped back to allow Des to shut the doors of his van.

"I'm sure our paths will cross again soon. Until that happens, I'll wish you a good day and an enjoyable weekend."

"We've decided to work through the weekend, you see, we're doing our utmost to find the killer."

"Glad you haven't let me down. Have a good one, and wishing you all the success you need to find this sick and twisted fucker."

"Thanks, I have an idea we're going to need it."

CHAPTER 10

*H*e woke up and rubbed the gunge out of his eyes. He'd had the worst night's sleep in a long time. His thoughts rampant, along with the voices. All in all, everything was driving him to distraction, to the point of him regretting his actions. He'd only started because of the voices urging him to break out of his mundane existence. It had been that way since she'd left him. He detested his life, it was nothing compared to the one he'd had with her. But being out in the fields all day, working from four in the morning until ten at night during the summer had been the cause of their marriage unravelling, without him even real-ising it.

He shook his head to dislodge the memories. She was gone now, she'd made her choice. Anger seared his veins. He cobbled together some breakfast for his prisoner. He'd feed her, have some fun with her, and then go hunting for a companion to keep her company.

Oh yes, what an excellent idea that is, and without me prompting you as well. You're getting better at this fiendish behaviour. I'm proud of you and what you've become lately. I'd like to take credit for helping you achieve your new motivation.

"Whatever. It was a long time coming. What should I give her to eat? Perhaps I should knock up some porridge. It was probably cold out there in the barn last night. I forgot to leave her a blanket."

Doh, in this weather, are you mad? No, don't respond, we all know the answer to that one.

Laughter filled his confused mind. He poured some oats into a bowl, added milk and put it in the microwave for a minute, removed it from the oven, stirred it and popped it back in for a further minute. Then he poured the contents into a deep dish and chopped up the last banana he had sitting in the fruit bowl.

Looks like gruel to me... I bet she doesn't ask for more.

"Shut up, it's a perfectly good plate of food, I'd eat it. Maybe I'll tuck into it myself if she turns her nose up at it."

He made the woman a mug of tea and added a spoonful of sugar, despite not knowing if that's the way she preferred to drink it. He'd finish that off as well if she rejected it.

The barn door was still secured. There was no reason why it shouldn't have been, but he wondered if that had caused him concern during the night and why he'd failed to grab any sleep.

The woman was awake and eased herself up onto her elbow but collapsed again, too weak to hold herself upright for long against the restraints holding her in place. A tinge of guilt gnawed at his stomach. It only lasted a few seconds, and then it was gone again. He really couldn't give a shit if she was struggling or not. She wouldn't be hanging around long anyway. He was still toying with the idea of getting in touch with her husband about a ransom. Half of him wanted to put the house right with the funds and the other half couldn't be bothered going down that route and dealing with the hassle it was likely to bring his way.

"Here, are you hungry?"

The woman stared at him, not moving a muscle.

"I asked you a question, I'm giving you permission to speak now. Oops, I suppose I should take the rag out of your mouth first." He removed the cloth and helped her to sit upright.

She moistened her lips and whispered, "Why are you doing this to me? What do you want?"

"I want you to eat your breakfast. Did you sleep well?"

She shook her head. "No, not with that thing stuck in my mouth. I thought it was going to choke me."

"Ah, yes, I slipped up. I should have placed tape over your mouth instead, like they do on the TV. I'm still new to all of this, learning on the job as it were."

"But why? Why are you doing this to me?"

"Why not? Because I can. Do you want this grub or not?"

"Not. I don't want anything from you. All I want is to go home to my family." She kicked out and caught him in the shin.

The move was unexpected, and he no longer had the sharp reflexes he used to possess to jump out of the way. He placed the bowl on the bale beside her and struck her around the face, first one side and then the other. "You ungrateful bitch. You're going to regret treating me like that. I'm going to make you suffer more now. I've changed my plans for you. Bitches like you need to be taught a lesson, and I'm going to be the one to do that to you."

Her head sank into the bale of hay behind her. "No, I'm sorry, I won't do it again, I promise."

"Forgive me if I don't believe you. People like you are born liars. Now, do you want this meal I've prepared for you or not?"

"Not. I hate porridge at the best of times. It's prison food."

He tipped his head back and laughed. "Maybe you need to look around you and take in the fix you're in, love."

She gulped and shook her head. "Why are you doing this?" she repeated. "Why won't you tell me?"

"Hey, you need to be thankful I ain't killed you… yet. The other two pissed me off within seconds, forcing me to end their lives."

"But I don't want to die."

"Tell me who does, no one I know. Even the animals I've slaughtered over the years had fear in their eyes when they saw the blade coming at them."

"How could you kill an animal?"

"Easily." He withdrew the large butcher's knife from the back of his jeans and held it to her chained throat. "One swift slice, and it'll be all over within a second or two. Of course, there's been the odd occasion when I've screwed up and the sheep escaped my clutches, only to run around in circles, collapse and die from its wounds minutes later. If it hadn't struggled in the first place it would have died without the extra pain and needless suffering. Something for you to keep in mind."

She nodded. "I won't make a fuss. I'm willing to do anything and everything you want me to."

He cocked an eyebrow and grinned. "Really? Is that so? Hmm… I'd better get my thinking cap on, see what games I can come up with to entice you to play with me, not that you'll have the option."

"Please, all I want is to be with my family. If it means I have to give myself to you in order to achieve that, then so be it."

"Hark at you. Who said I wanted to take advantage of you anyway? Maybe I've got far better things to do with my time than spend it in here with you, teaching you a lesson on how to respect those of us who you deem beneath you."

"When have I given you that impression? I never judge people, it's not in my nature to do it. Please, I have a family, my son is in his second year of university. I want to be around to see what career he chooses at the end of his course."

"Lucky him. My career was set in stone when I was in nappies, to run this place, a thriving farm, until…"

She inclined her head. "Until? What happened? I've been told I have a good ear and a willing shoulder for people to cry on."

"Bully for you. I don't need any sympathy, stop thinking I do. And stop believing you know what's best for me, you don't. Only I know that, so sod off. Last chance, do you want your breakfast or not?"

"No, I'd rather starve."

"If that's the way you want it. It shouldn't take long, it's not like you've got a lot of flesh on them bones of yours, is it?"

"I keep myself trim through diet and exercise. I cycle everywhere."

"You need to be more aware of your surroundings when you're cycling. I hear there are some right nutters out there, ready to pounce at a moment's notice."

"I usually do. You caught me unawares, sorting out the bikes while Paul had to run to use the loo in the café. Someone will have seen you. It's only a matter of time before the police come knocking on your door."

"Bring it on. I'll be ready for them. I've got a number of guns in the house, all loaded, ready for action. I'm not afraid of them. I'm not scared of going out at this stage in my life. I've had my share of dealing with selfish people like you."

She frowned. "You don't know me, so how can you call

me selfish? I'm far from it. My husband helps to run a charity, and I assist him with fundraising events now and again. Selfish? Not me, not by a long shot."

"All right, maybe that was a mistake on my part. Whatever, who gives a shit? I don't. Anyway, I don't have to stand around here, justifying myself to you, not when I have a lot to do. My day is always full."

"Doing what? I can't hear any animals around here."

"Stop questioning me. You haven't got a clue how I occupy my days, and I have no intention of sharing the details with you."

"Are you struggling to make ends meet? I heard a story on the news only last week that farmers are dealing with financial ruin, mainly due to climate change. You can seek out support from the government. They're willing to dish out funds to farmers who are in desperate need, to prevent them from going under."

Her statement made him pause and think.

Hey, she might be onto something there. You could ask, there's no harm in that. They might fund the repairs to that gable end, who knows? But you're going to need to get on the blower or the website to find out... and you're crap at doing things like that. Maybe she can help you. Yes, get her to fill out the forms for you. You can give her the impression that you'll be willing to let her go, and once she's completed the forms you can kill her. Job done, over and out. See ya later, baby!

"I couldn't do that, could I?"

"Of course you can," the woman replied. "I'm even prepared to help you. It's no problem. I help people with online stuff all the time."

"You'd be prepared to do that for me? Why?"

"Because I believe you're out of your depth here. I don't think you intended kidnapping me, did you?"

Don't listen to her! I'm warning you, listen to her instead of me and it'll be your downfall, mate.

He slapped her around the face again, on both cheeks. She screamed out, her head thrashing one way and then the other.

"Don't mess with my head. I've got enough going on up there as it is, without you having a go as well."

She sobbed. Snot dribbled from her nose. "I'm sorry. I didn't mean... I was only trying to help."

He picked up the cereal bowl and the mug of tea and left the barn. It wasn't until he was outside that he realised he hadn't shoved the cloth back in her mouth. He returned to do it and marched towards her with intent. She cowered away from him, sending a thrill shooting through his veins. The power, it was all-consuming.

I could get used to this.

He laughed and left the barn again, without a second glance over his shoulder. He was on yet another mission, and nothing would stand in his way.

CHAPTER 11

 aturday

THE SEARCH for Lisa Mayer had been relentless, and not a single clue had come their way so far. Even finding her phone and the knife hadn't produced the results they were hoping for. Yes, there was a fingerprint or two on the case, plus a single one on the knife, but nothing had matched any possible suspects listed on the system.

"What the heck? Where the bloody hell do we look now?" Sam said as soon as she received the news from Claire. Sam had been scouring the outskirts of the village with the rest of her team since first light at around eight that morning, which had also proved to be a significant waste of time.

"It's obvious the killer is doing everything he can to mess with our heads," Claire suggested.

"Had you said that at the beginning of the week I would have poured water over that notion, but now... after giving the investigation our all over the past few days and still coming up with zilch, I'm inclined to agree with you, but why? Could the culprit be known to us?"

Claire took that as a hint to fire up the system. "It's not something I've delved into yet. It'll be a long job, going through every name in the village, but like you say, what other option do we have open to us?"

Sam nodded and patted Claire on the shoulder. "If you need another pair of hands, or eyes, give me a shout. In the meantime, we'll finish off our lunch and get back out there. If this morning is anything to go by, I think this afternoon is going to be hectic, with tourists either driving, riding, or even traipsing through the village."

"Making our job a whole lot harder to cope with," Bob grumbled. He picked up his cup and downed the rest of his drink, then reached for the last bite of his coffee-and-walnut cake which Emma had kindly made for them.

"At least the café is now covered, what with Emma getting her friend to install a temporary camera, overlooking the entrance and car park. That's a blessing and one less place to worry about."

"Yeah, she did good. It'll make our job a lot easier if the killer was expressly targeting this place," Bob stated.

Sam frowned and shuffled to the edge of her seat. "What makes you think that? There has only been the one occasion where anything has happened on site."

"Don't listen to me then if you think I'm talking a load of shit," he bit back defensively.

Sam shook her head. "Did I say you were talking shit? It was a genuine question. What are you getting at? If you can answer me without getting mardy, that would be a bonus."

"It's something I've been considering for a while. The first victim, Patricia, had arranged to meet her girlfriend here. The second vic, Anita, was a regular punter at The Gather. The third one, Lisa, was taken from outside the café, under everyone's noses. Is it just me who has picked up on the link? Maybe it is."

Sam shrugged and nibbled on her lip as she contemplated his suggestion. "Okay, I'm willing to play along with you on your theory, except to add a word of caution, to stop us getting ahead of ourselves."

"Which is?"

"That this is the only café in the village, scrap that, for miles in the area. Therefore, anyone likely to visit the lake, either by foot or on a bike, is bound to earmark this place as a meeting point."

"If you say so. I still don't think you should dismiss an obvious connection, you know, just because Emma is a friend of yours."

"I'm not, and there are ways of saying things. Your tone is way off the mark for me, partner."

"Sorry. I just think you're overlooking something obvious and it's not like you to be so…"

"Come on, Bob, don't hold back if you have something on your mind. Let's have it, all of it." Sam's blood flowed faster, red hot, searing her veins.

Bob wiped a hand over his face, clearly nervous about opening his mouth and letting utter tripe fall out of it. "I was merely pointing out that maybe we should do some digging into the café's history, that's all."

Sam held her palms up. "And that's it? How do you propose we do that?"

"I'm not with you. The usual way, of course. Ask around, see what dirt we can dig up."

"If anything," she added swiftly. "I'm going to do better than that."

"Go on, what do you intend doing?"

"I'm going downstairs to have a chat with Emma, not that I haven't done that already, when we first arrived in fact. Just adding that for the record, you know, in case you think I've been neglecting my duties in any shape or form."

Bob sighed and folded his arms. "And you wonder why I have a tendency to keep my mouth shut most of the time."

Sam laughed and swiped his arm. "This grumpy old man syndrome doesn't suit you, just saying."

"If I'm *grumpy* it's because I've gone without my usual lie-in on a Saturday morning, for what? To sit around here, twiddling our fingers and for you to have a go at me, shoot me down in flames for suggesting something that should have been obvious right at the start of the investigation."

"Stop right there before you say something even more offensive. Just to appease you, I'm going to go downstairs and have a chat with *my friend*, Emma, now. And here's another snippet of information that may have escaped your notice. She's also given up her day off today to be here for us. She usually only works Monday to Friday."

Bob sank lower into his chair and was wise enough to keep his mouth shut.

Sam collected the plates and the empty cups and saucers that were dotted around and stacked them on a tray. She picked it up and headed towards the door.

Bob called out, "Watch you don't trip up on your way down."

"You can be so childish when you don't get a lie-in," she shouted over her shoulder, carefully minding her step as she proceeded down the steeper-than-normal staircase.

After leaving the tray on the counter, Sam made her way over to the office and knocked on the door. Emma looked up and gestured for her to join her. She was mid-call and invited Sam to take a seat.

Sam glanced around the office at the schedules pinned on the board in front of Emma. Her friend had always been the super organised one at school.

Emma ended the call and breathed out a heavy sigh. "Sorry about that. Trouble with a supplier, one that we've just got involved with."

"Ugh… you can do without the hassle, right? This place must be a goldmine."

"It has its moments. The café is always busy, rarely an empty table most days, and the craft items, made by the locals, all appear to sell well, so I suppose we mustn't grumble. How's the investigation going, Sam? It must be so frustrating for you and your team not to have found the killer by now. How do you deal with the huge wave of disappointment washing over you most days, or shouldn't I ask?"

"Most of the time we've got something concrete to go on; however, nothing could be further from the truth this time. I know the village is only small, but the sheer volume of tourists visiting the area, well, that's where the challenge lies for us."

"I can imagine. I'd hate to be in your shoes. Can I say how impressed I've been with you and your team since you've arrived here?"

"Oh, any reason?"

"You haven't disrupted us in the slightest, especially the café. I'll be forever grateful for that. As the nights draw in, trade always gets slower. If you think this time of year is busy with tourists, you need to pay a visit during July and August. On second thoughts, I wouldn't bother, it can be a nightmare and a definite challenge most days."

"I bet. Once we pack up our bags and leave here, I'm definitely going to be a regular visitor at the weekends. Rhys agreed when he popped over with the dogs the other night."

"We're always up for having more regulars, especially if they have four-legged companions with them."

Sam's mouth dried up as she searched for the right words. In the end, she decided to jump in feet first. "I know I asked the question when we first showed up here, but a lot has happened since then, so it might be worth mentioning it again."

"Am I missing something? Mentioning what?"

"Sorry if that all sounded like gobbledygook. My team and I have been bouncing around a few ideas upstairs, whilst tucking into your fabulous sandwiches—I know, I'm a creep. And my partner came up with the suggestion... hear me out... that maybe the crimes committed this week might somehow be connected to this place."

Emma's head jutted forward. "Well, I don't see how. Any specific reason behind you thinking that?"

"Only the fact that the victims were either on their way here or had stopped by and used this place regularly."

"And that's it?" Emma scratched the side of her head. "What do you expect me to say to that, Sam?"

"Nothing, not really. Emma, it's not an accusation. All I'm trying to do, in my ham-fisted way, is figure out if there's some kind of connection to The Gather. Can you think of any?"

"No, absolutely and categorically not. God, how awful and totally inappropriate of you to think that way."

Sam regretted opening her mouth, seeing the pain etched into Emma's face. She rested a hand on her friend's forearm. "It was a dumb idea. I didn't mean to upset you, love."

"But you went ahead and said it anyway. That's unforgivable. I'm mortified you should even consider that notion."

"It's all we've got to go on right now. The investigation is tying us up in knots, and a member of my team chucked that idea into the hat."

"You could have dismissed it, though, what with you being the one in charge, couldn't you?"

"You're right, I could, and should, have done that, without a second thought. I apologise."

"It doesn't matter. Actually, I probably got angry because you're not the only one to consider the idea. It's been turning over and over in my mind all week. I have to say, I haven't been able to work out if there could be something to it or not. You've seen how we operate around here; all the staff are friendly. If they're not, they're immediately shown the door. I'm no pushover, I promise you. I've never knowingly fallen out with any of the locals, maybe a few choice words here and there with people complaining the bins aren't dealt with and are cluttering up the car park, once they've been emptied, you know how annoying bin men can be when they want to be. But surely, taking that on board, it wouldn't piss someone off enough for them to consider taking revenge on my customers, or would it? You tell me, you're the detective. You're the one used to dealing with deranged characters day in and day out."

"No, I don't think that's likely, Emma. I didn't mean to cause offence, that wasn't my intention at all. I'm sorry."

"Don't be. It's over and done with as far as I'm concerned, no ill-feelings."

"Thanks, I'd hate it if we fell out about this."

"We won't. Sorry, was there anything else? Only I have a few calls I need to make. I'm trying to get ahead for the week as I have a funeral to attend on Thursday."

"Sorry to hear that. Thinking about it, I've got one I need to attend on Friday, myself." Sadness inched its way through Sam's insides to settle in her heart.

"I know, love. She'd want you there. All this must be keeping you going, though, am I right?"

"It's definitely serving as a distraction. Probably pissing off my family in the process."

"Everyone has their own way of dealing with grief. We shouldn't sit and mourn, we should celebrate a loved one's passing, that's how your mother would have wanted it, isn't it?"

"I've never really thought about it like that before. Maybe you're right. I know I've had a few sleepless nights since her death, feeling guilty for not breaking down and sobbing."

"Aww... you mustn't think that way, Sam. I'm sure your grief will hit you eventually, probably when you least expect it. It doesn't mean that you thought any less of your mother when she was alive. Be kind to yourself. Life goes on. It's for living, not for having regrets."

Emma leaned over with her arms outstretched, and Sam fell into them, struggling to hold it together.

A knock sounded on the door, and they swiftly parted. Sam glanced over her shoulder to see Bob gesticulating with his arms that he needed to see her.

"It looks urgent, I'd better see what he wants. Although, he can be a bit of a drama queen at times, but those words have never left my mouth."

Emma stifled a laugh behind a fake cough.

Sam opened the door and asked, "Bob, is there something you need?"

"Yes. You. Pronto. Out front." He turned his back on her and bolted towards the exit.

Sam faced Emma and shrugged. "I think I'm needed. I'll see you later."

"Good luck. Hope it's nothing too serious to deal with."

"So do I," Sam mumbled.

Outside, Liam and Oliver were comforting a young woman in the car park. Bob was anxiously peering over his shoulder, waiting for Sam to join him.

He approached her and said in a low voice, "Her friend has gone missing."

"Shit. Where? When?"

"If you'll let me finish, I'll fill you in with all the details."

"I apologise. Carry on."

"The young lady is Violet Hodges; her friend, Nicky Clarke. You might recall us speaking with them during our stay at the Fox and Hounds? Anyhow, Nicky went out for a stroll around the village a couple of hours ago and hasn't been seen since."

"Bugger. Yes, I remember chatting to them in the bar the other night. They're from Devon if my memory serves me right. Shit. I take it Violet has tried calling Nicky?"

"Yes, it's the first thing she did. She's been trying to contact her every ten minutes or so. It's not looking good, Sam."

"Let's not get carried away with this and get ourselves worked up, not yet, Bob. We need to try and retrace Nicky's steps around the village. Did Violet give any indication in which direction Nicky set off?"

"No. Nicky needed to make a call to her husband, something about their dog going to the vet's for a small operation and she was concerned about its welfare. Want me to check if she placed that call?"

"Yes, that should be our first priority."

Bob and Sam joined the small group.

"Shall we take this round the back, out of earshot of the locals?" Sam suggested.

Violet was distraught. Her hands shook as she flicked back a clump of her long blonde hair behind her left ear. "Please, you can't delay the search. I don't know how long she's been missing. Discussing it further is only going to prove detrimental, isn't it?"

"Just a brief chat. We need to get an idea of what we're dealing with first, before we can put a plan into action."

Sam led the way, the wind cutting through her when she turned the corner, but it died down again once they were

181

seated at the picnic table outside the café. "Right, when did Nicky set off?"

"Around twelve, I think. She wanted to ring Guy, and then we were going to head up here for a bite to eat."

Bob and Sam glanced at each other, and her partner hitched up a shoulder as if to say, 'I told you so'.

Sam ignored him and asked, "And you've tried calling her mobile?"

"Yes, dozens of times. The more I try, the more frustrated I'm becoming. Frustrated and scared. I've heard the gossip circulating the village. We're due to go home tomorrow, we both have to be back at work on Monday."

"Let's try and remain calm. We'll organise another search party to look for her. What I need you to do is keep trying her number for us. Does it generally ring out or go straight to voicemail?"

"It keeps ringing, that's the part I can't get my head around."

"You said she left the pub to ring her husband. Can you give us his number?"

She opened her phone and showed Sam the number. Sam rang it, and a man answered a few seconds later.

"Hello, is this Guy Clarke?"

"It is. Who wants to know?"

"Sorry to disturb you. I'm DI Sam Cobbs. I'm investigating several crimes that have taken place this week up at Ennerdale Bridge, the village where your wife is staying with her friend, Violet."

"I'm well aware of where my wife is at this time, Inspector. How can I help?"

"I'm here with Violet, and she's told us that Nicky left the pub to go on a walk. She was going to check in with you about how your dog is getting on after its operation. Have you heard from Nicky?"

"Yes, she rang a while ago to see how Coco was. She's fine by the way. I don't understand what you're getting at, isn't Nicky with you?"

Sam inhaled a steadying breath. "Unfortunately not. Violet has been out searching for her. I'm afraid at this point, we're unsure about what has happened to Nicky. Hence my calling you."

"My God, what are you saying? That Nicky is now on the missing list?"

"That would appear to be the case. I'm sorry. We're organising another search and intend to keep looking for your wife until we find her."

"Good to hear. Give me half an hour to arrange for Coco to stay with my mother and I'll get on the road. I insist on being part of the search, if, as you presume, my wife has gone missing. Jesus, this is unbelievable. She told me the police presence in the village is phenomenal, it doesn't make sense for her to go missing if you guys are crawling all over the area."

"I'm sorry, sir. If you want to travel up here then that's your prerogative. Personally, I would leave it a few hours. I can arrange for a member of my team to contact you at say four, if we haven't managed to locate her by then."

"Whatever, that'll give me time to get things sorted down here. Do your best to find her, Inspector, she's all I've got, well, her and Coco, and there's something else you should know."

Sam closed her eyes, sensing what he was about to say next. "What's that?"

"She's eight weeks pregnant, not that anyone has been told about the baby yet."

"Okay, your secret is safe with me. I know words are cheap in these circumstances, but please, try not to worry too much. There are several officers out there, already searching for your wife."

"I should hope so. Ring me at four. In the meantime, I'll pack a bag and call my mother."

"I'll be in touch soon." Sam ended the call.

"She's pregnant? I had a feeling that was the case, she's been in the loo most mornings, being sick. I didn't query it with her, thought I'd keep my nose out until she plucked up the courage to share the news with me," Violet said. She covered her face with her hands and sobbed.

Sam threw an arm around her shoulder and gestured for the others to leave them alone for a moment. "I'm sorry you had to overhear that news. We're going to give it our all to find Nicky and her unborn child. Please, don't give up on us."

"She doesn't deserve this. What if... we don't get her back? What if she ends up... like the others? I won't be able to forgive myself for letting her go off on her own like that... I should have gone with her. It was a silly, naïve mistake for both of us to make, given what's going on in the village right now."

Sam sighed. "You can't blame yourself. Look around you, there are dozens of officers on duty in the village, no one would think it possible for the perpetrator to strike again so soon."

"Who is this person? Do you know where the other woman is? The possible third victim? Has she shown up yet... or her body?" Her voice trailed off at the end.

"No, neither. We need to acknowledge that as a positive right now. The less we hear the better at this stage."

"I think I understand your reasoning behind that statement. Oh God, what if the person who is holding her, tortures her and she loses the baby? They've tried for years to get pregnant. If she loses it now, she'll be devastated, if she comes out of this situation alive."

"You mustn't even contemplate whether Nicky will come through this alive or not. I tend to deal in positive outcomes not negative ones. For your own peace of mind, I believe you should be doing the same." Sam was chomping at the bit to get back to her team, to get the ball rolling rather than going over old ground with Violet, who was intent on blaming herself.

CHAPTER 12

*H*e knew he'd taken a risk, abducting the woman in the centre of the village. The voices had urged him to take the gamble, and thankfully it had paid off. He'd grabbed her; she'd been distracted as most people are these days, studying her confounded social media on her phone. He'd slapped the tape over her mouth, knocked her out cold and shoved her in the back seat of his car, adrenaline fuelling every strategic movement. Here she was, still out cold, lying on a bale of straw next to the other woman.

"I need to get your name," he said to his first captive. He removed the rag from her mouth.

"It's Lisa, Lisa Mayer."

He tore off a piece of tape and secured her mouth. She bucked, obviously aware how painful it was likely to be if he chose to remove it in the future.

"Don't worry, it won't hurt, not much, not that you're going to be around long enough to suffer, not if I have my way." He rubbed his hands together and did a little jig around the barn, the voices cheering him on and rejoicing at his triumphs.

A noise outside caught his attention.

Shit! Are we expecting anyone?

"No one has been here for a while. Fuck, I need to see who it is and play it cool." He fixed a smile in place and opened the door of the barn which he closed immediately behind him. His heart raced, and he was thankful that he'd secured both women's mouths with tape. "Hello, there, how can I help?"

Two men in dark suits got out of a grey Kia Sportage and were facing the farmhouse. They turned and waved. One of them flashed an ID when they got to within a few feet of him.

"Are you Jim Kirk? We're Detective Constables O'Callahan and Lucas. Would it be possible to have a word with you?" Lucas said. The man on the right had pointed out who was who as he'd introduced them.

"Of course, about anything in particular?"

"I presume you're aware the police have been in the area all week," Lucas said. "We're making general enquiries with the locals, asking if they may have witnessed anything unusual going on close to where they live."

"Ah, my neighbour at the end of the lane said someone had stopped to speak with him a few days ago. I thought it was strange that no one had dropped by to see me. Still, this place is a bit tucked away off the road, I suppose. I'm sorry, I have to say I've seen nothing. In fact, I've barely set foot off the farm in a couple of weeks." He gave them one of his notoriously friendly smiles, showing off his solitary tooth at the front. "I've been up to my neck in preparing the farm and the animals for winter, you know, stocking up on the essentials, like food. It's surprising how much the bloody cows and sheep eat, despite the grass being lush and green at this time of year."

"I'm sure," Lucas said. "Well, if you haven't seen anyone

suspicious hanging around, we won't hold you up any longer, Mr Kirk. Thank you for your time. Are there any other farms or houses up this way?"

"No, my farm is the last one in the village. It's all farmland and fells beyond this, now."

Lucas smiled, and both men jumped back into the vehicle. Jim stayed perfectly still, his smile never fading, not until the Kia had left his drive, then he tore open the barn again and marched towards the two women. Lisa shied away from him, fearful of his stance, no doubt, and the other woman was beginning to stir. He kicked her leg. She opened her eyes and stared at him and then took in her surroundings. Bound at the wrists and the ankles, she struggled to sit upright, and tears sprang to her eyes when she saw Lisa sitting a few feet away from her.

"Nice of you to join us. This is Lisa. As you can see, she's in the same predicament as you. I'll tell you the same thing I told her when she arrived: do as you're told and you won't get hurt, not yet. Got that?"

The younger woman nodded.

"What's your name?"

She mumbled something behind the tape.

Stupid! How the heck are you going to hear what she says with the tape slapped over her mouth? You can be such a dickhead when you want to be.

"Shut up," he mumbled and tore the tape from her mouth, but only for long enough to allow her to speak.

"It's Nicky. Nicky Clarke. Please, why are you doing this? I don't have any money. My husband and I aren't wealthy at all. I'm here for a week's holiday with my…."

He'd heard enough and secured her mouth with the same piece of tape, catching her mid-sentence. She twisted her head from side to side, making it difficult to find the target at first until his fist caught her in the stomach. That made her stop dead in her tracks. Her eyes widened. It sounded as though she was shouting something at him from behind the tape.

"Shut up! You don't speak until I ask you a question, you hear me?"

Nicky had the sense to keep quiet after that. He took several steps back to study both women as the voices in his head started up again. Each one giving him what they assumed to be useful advice which only seemed to make him more confused with every passing second.

He filled his lungs with air and shouted, "SHUT UP!"

The women glanced at each other, their eyes blazing with fear as he took not one but two steps closer to Lisa. She turned her head away from him, but it made no odds. His hands slid easily around her slim throat. He choked her until her eyes bulged and then released her. She struggled to breathe behind the tape but somehow, she managed it. The voices prompted him, willing him to finish her off, but the thrill rippling through him had given him another buzz that he was keen to sense again.

He took a step to his left and, with his hands outstretched towards Nicky's throat, his gaze latched on to hers. She bucked, used all her strength to tumble sideways in an attempt to evade his weathered, gnarled hands. But due to her restraints, her movements were limited. Sensing she had to fight in order to survive, she kicked out with her bound legs, painfully bending his knee back. Instantly, he felt something snap, either a ligament or a tendon. The agony intensified within seconds to an unbearable level.

"You fucking bitch, you're going to pay for that."

Lisa had other ideas. She came to the younger woman's defence and kicked his thigh several times. He backed away and hobbled back and forth across the floor, needing time to think about how to proceed. Both women had pissed him off and now deserved to be punished. He didn't care if the retribution he dished out ended their lives.

CHAPTER 13

*E*veryone in the village was out there, doing their utmost to find the latest missing woman; however, there were certain members of the community who Sam got the impression were beginning to rebel. Unfortunately, it was poor Emma who was taking the brunt of their frustrations. Once or twice throughout the afternoon, Sam had needed to step in and defuse a heated discussion between the locals and Emma, leaving Emma feeling distraught and downright miserable.

Sam took her to one side after one such confrontation. "My advice would be to close the café and go home, love. I'm sensing that word is getting around and the natives are restless, wanting their pound of flesh... from you."

"But why me? What the heck do I have to do with this? Do you believe they're thinking along the lines of what you said earlier? You know, that The Gather, or possibly I, could be the key to this mad person striking all the time? God, I hope not. I couldn't cope, knowing that was hanging over my head."

"The truth is, I don't know what to believe any longer,

Emma. But I feel it's my job to try and keep you safe, therefore, I would close the café and go home, just to avoid getting involved in any more confrontations with your neighbours."

"Whilst I agree with you, getting away from a toxic atmosphere, won't some people read into it, come across as me being guilty of something? I haven't got the foggiest."

Sam paused to contemplate her question. "Maybe. I wish I had a clear-cut answer for you, but I haven't."

Just then, Lucas pulled up alongside Sam, outside the café. He lowered his window. "That's definitely all the locals questioned now, boss. We've just stopped out at Jim Kirk's place. He was tending to his animals in the barn when we got there, seemed surprised to see us. He said his farm was the final property up that lane and that he hadn't seen anyone suspicious hanging around out there."

"Sorry to interrupt," Emma said. "You're talking about toothless Jim? I can't remember his surname."

"That's right. The last house down by the lake. He said there was nothing but farmland and the fells beyond him," Lucas replied.

Emma's brow wrinkled, and her head shook. "He doesn't have any animals. Last I heard, he was in the process of selling up. You know him, Sam, Jim was here, in the café, the day the news broke about the first victim, her body being found in the forest. He actually helped with the search."

Sam closed her eyes and tried to envisage the man Emma was referring to. "I think I remember him. Yes, he was one of the first people I interviewed. He told me himself that he'd sold off all his flock. What are you saying, Oliver, that you thought he looked a bit shifty?"

He shrugged. "No, not in the slightest, but he did leave the barn pretty much as soon as we arrived."

"Do you think it warrants a further visit? If, as Emma has

said, he doesn't have any animals left on the farm, why would he feel the need to lie about that?"

"What's this?" Bob asked. He'd just emerged from the café, having used the facilities.

"We don't have time to explain. We'll take two cars. I'm going to arrange for a few uniformed officers to join us."

"Is someone going to tell me what the hell is going on?" Bob asked childishly.

Sam's mind raced. *Here we are in the middle of nowhere, no Tasers to hand.* "Emma, I would shut up shop for the day, as I've already suggested."

"I'm reluctant to do it but I think you're right. Bloody hell, Jim Kirk, I would never have put him in the frame." Her friend wandered inside and hung the Closed sign on the front door.

"Before we set off, I'm going to need his address, Oliver. None of us are armed. I'm going to make the call and get an ART out here."

"Why?" Bob asked, his frustration kicking in.

Sam took a few moments to reveal what they were up against.

"Jesus, if it's the guy I think you're talking about, he's been hanging around here like a bad penny at times. Didn't he lend a hand on a couple of the searches?"

Sam nodded. "That's the one. Fucking weirdo, he's been sticking close beside us, no doubt laughing at us, striking, abducting the women when we least expected him to, aware of where we were the whole time. That's how he's remained a couple of steps ahead of us."

Moments later, Emma came tearing out of the café and ran towards them. "Hey, before you set off, I've just had a word with Helen. She's reminded me that Jim was married up until a few years ago. His wife went off with a tourist who often came to the café during his stays at the Fox and Hounds."

"Shit, really? That would explain him targeting not only the punters visiting the café but the customers staying at the pub, too. So, his motive is to take revenge on the tourists coming to the area?" Sam queried, perplexed.

"How do you work that one out when all the victims have been females?" Bob asked.

"A heart broken by a woman, he's been killing two birds with one stone, punishing female tourists. Warped way of thinking about it, but it's a possibility nonetheless," Sam pointed out.

"There's more to the story," Emma interrupted them.

"Go on," Sam said, intrigued.

"His wife and this fella she took off with... they both died."

"What? How?"

"He was an experienced fell-walker. She reportedly went on a hike with him, somewhere up near Penrith. Their bodies were found after they took a tumble from one of the sheer drops up there. The story was in the newspaper. Jesus, Jim was devastated by the news. Christ, we even had a whip-round for him. The whole village took pity on him for her treating him like shit, and now this..."

"Okay, Emma, I'm going to need you to keep this information close to your chest for the time being. We'll shoot out there and see where the land lies. Go home, just in case things get a little hairy around here and he finds his way back to the café. I'm not saying that could be on the agenda, but it's better to be cautious."

"Gosh, yes. I'm going to kick the punters out now. I've never had to sink to that level before. There's a chance it might damage our business, but when the Devil comes knocking, eh? And I need to keep all my staff safe. Once we receive word that he's been arrested, I'll come back here and clear up later."

"I'll ring you as and when I have any further news. Take care, love, and thanks for the information, you're a star."

"All in a day's work as they say. I'll pass on your thanks to Helen, she has her uses." Emma smiled and gave Sam a brief hug. "Good luck."

"Thanks. Keep your wits about you, Emma. I'd hate it if anything happened to you."

"It won't. I shouldn't say this, but I keep a cricket bat in the office, behind the door, you know, in case of emergencies. TTFN." Administering that stark revelation, Emma trotted back to the café and smiled at Sam through the glass pane in the front door.

Sam was left shaking her head. Bob nudged her with his elbow.

"You think we should get the ball rolling? I would think there's a lot to organise, in one way or another."

"Yes, absolutely. Where would I be without you pointing out the obvious all the time, partner?"

Bob stepped away, chuntering expletives under his breath. Sam fished her phone out of her pocket and then reconsidered. Instead, she went to the bottom of the stairs and called up for Claire to join them.

The second she laid eyes on Claire, she said, "Can you arrange for an ART to join us out at Jim Kirk's farm? We're heading out there to assess the situation. They can join us and make their move as soon as they arrive. Until then, we'll keep the farm under surveillance, pounce if we feel it's necessary."

"I'll get on it right away, boss. Keep in touch. If I can do anything else at this end, give me a shout."

"Don't worry, I will." Sam waved and then collected her

partner from his sulking area around the back of The Gather. "Come on, Mardy Pants."

"I can do without you having a pop at me in front of the others. There are rules about that kind of harassment in your handbook. You might want to take a refresher course on it from time to time."

Sam sank onto the bench opposite him. "Hey, it was a joke. My way of dealing with the tension this investigation has heaped on my shoulders. I'll keep my mouth buttoned in future and do things by the book instead."

"No, you're all right. It's me being oversensitive, as usual. Sorry, Sam, you have enough on your plate without me throwing my dummy out of the pram."

Sam smiled and patted his hand. "You said it. Come on, Bugalugs, we've got a killer to catch."

SAM INSISTED on following Oliver out to the location. They pulled up in a lay-by close to the farm, and Oliver and Liam jumped in the back seat of Sam's car, where they ran through the final details of the planned swoop, if one was called for, before the ART arrived.

So, Bob and I will take the lead. I'm only saying that because I want to tackle Kirk head-on. I think it will put him in a spin, a woman being in charge."

"You could be right," Bob added. "Do we know how long the ART is going to be?"

"No, can someone ring Claire to check?"

"I will," Liam said, already dialling the sergeant's number. "Claire, it's Liam. We're outside the farm. What's the ETA on the ART?" He put his phone on speaker, and Claire's voice filled the car.

"They told me they would get on the road ASAP. Reckon they should be here within the hour."

"Shit, that's going to seem like an eternity to us, sitting here, twiddling our damn thumbs," Bob complained.

"I agree. I'm making the call to get in there, who's with me? Bearing in mind we haven't got any Tasers to hand."

"Each arrest is different. If we have to do things the old-fashioned way, I'm up for it," Liam said.

"I don't wish to jump up and down on anyone's enthusiasm here, but I think you're forgetting this bloke has killed two women already, more for all we know. He's a farmer who has probably got guns on his land..." Bob stated, doing his best to keep their feet on the ground.

"You're right. We should take nothing for granted," Sam agreed, "however, if you'd rather wait, then I'll have to reluctantly go with you guys."

"I'm up for it," Liam and Oliver said in unison.

"Jesus," Bob muttered. "I suppose that leaves me outnumbered."

"You can stay in the car if you're that against it," Sam said, keen to make a move. "Claire, are you still there?"

"I am, boss."

"Send all the uniformed officers you can lay your hands on up here but tell them to hang back for the time being."

"Consider it done. You've got this, guys."

"Thanks," Sam replied.

With her pulse speeding through her veins, she opened the car door and stepped out of the vehicle. Her three colleagues did the same.

"Let's take a quick gander for now. If the mission seems beyond us then I'm willing to throw my hands up in the air and admit defeat, but while we believe he's holding two women hostage in there, I refuse to sit out here and do sod all."

"Then let's stop talking and get on with it," Bob urged.

They crossed the road. Sam had every intention of

staying well-hidden once they got close to the gateway of the farm, but when she heard shouting, all of her intended plans went out of the window.

"It sounds like it's coming from over there. Is that the barn he was coming out of when you visited him earlier?" Sam asked Liam and Oliver.

"Yes, the one on the right," Liam replied.

As Liam opened his mouth to reply, the barn door flew open and the man Sam recognised as 'helpful Jim' appeared, clutching his head and shouting. He was acting like a crazed animal. Spinning one way on the spot, stopping, then spinning in the opposite direction.

"What the fuck is that all about?" Bob asked. "Is he injured or what?"

"If I had to take a punt, I'd say he was having a psychotic episode," Sam whispered, her gaze never leaving the killer and the weirdness he was exhibiting.

"Happy fucking days, so he genuinely is a 'nutter' then?" Bob grumbled beside her.

"Let's see how this plays out for a second or two. Listen for any noises coming from inside the barn. All we've heard so far is *him* crying out. If he's got voices chuntering on in that head of his, this could turn into something unpredictable pretty darn quickly."

The four of them watched and waited until Jim eventually came to a standstill. He seemed to be in a complete daze, in a world of his own.

"He's confused, which could make him dangerous, or should I say more dangerous."

"I'm happy to leave things as they are and wait for the ART to arrive," Bob stated.

Sam issued a warning glance that shot him down in flames. "Nope, it isn't going to happen, Bob. Between us, I believe we can take him down. Study him carefully, tell me what you see."

"A fucker who has a toolbox for a head with more than a handful of screws jiggling around inside it."

Sam sighed. "Apart from that?"

Her partner shrugged. "Pass. You tell me."

"He hasn't got any weapons with him. I say we should strike, take advantage of that fact."

Bob chewed his lip. Sam could tell the notion was churning in his head. "It's your call."

"Okay, I say it's time to talk to his demons, whether he likes it or not." Sam stood from the crouching position she had adopted to assess the suspect. "Let's do this, gang."

Together, the four of them entered the driveway. Jim was none the wiser because he was facing the other way, staring at his farmhouse. Sam withdrew her warrant card from her pocket with her right hand and clutched the pepper spray in her left. She would have no hesitation in using it if things turned ugly. Glancing quickly towards the barn, she noticed the doors were firmly shut but not secured.

Are the two women in there? If so, what state are we going to find them in? Have they been tortured? Torn apart? Shredded limb from limb?

She refused to entertain the questions bombarding her mind and instead preferred to deal with the facts as they were presenting themselves to her.

Even the crunch of the gravel beneath their feet hadn't drawn Jim's attention.

"Jim Kirk," Sam shouted.

In a blind panic, Jim spun around to face them. "What the fuck? Who are you?" His eyes narrowed, and his gaze darted between the four of them and settled on Liam and Oliver. "I know you two, you were here earlier. I told you then I know nothing. I keep myself to myself in this village."

"Do you really, Jim?" Sam challenged. "Because I seem to

recall you assisting us at the beginning of our investigation. Why was that? To keep a close eye on what we were up to? Did you get a cheap thrill out of following our progress? Was that it?"

"I don't know what you're talking about. All I did was offer you lot a helping hand. Hell, you needed it. Hopeless you've been, absolutely hopeless."

"In your opinion, and yet, here we are, standing in your driveway. Where are the two women, Lisa and Nicky, Jim?"

He frowned and shrugged, but Sam also noticed a glint appear in his steel-grey eyes. "You tell me. Haven't you found them yet?"

"Okay, if you're determined to continue this futile game with us, you won't mind us having a nose around then, will you?"

His gaze automatically flitted to the barn, and he ran towards the door. Bob was the first to sprint after him. He brought Jim to his knees and secured his hands behind his back while Liam slapped on the handcuffs.

Unchallenged, Sam, with Oliver close behind her, inched open the door of the barn. Once her eyes adjusted to the darkness and she saw the two women trussed up, sitting on the straw, she bolted across the wide-open space with Oliver and proceeded to untie their hands and feet. Finally, Sam counted to three, and she and Oliver both ripped the tape from each of the women's mouths.

Tears of relief surfaced, and Lisa ran her tongue around her sore, chafed lips. "Thank God, you found us. Where is he? Is he likely to return and find you here?"

"No, he'll be sitting in the back of the car by now, don't worry, you're safe. We won't allow anything else to happen to you. Has he hurt you?"

Tears dripped onto the women's cheeks.

"No, not really," Nicky said. "Although he did punch me in the stomach, and I'm pregnant."

"Okay, we'll get you checked out at the hospital. It might be a good idea for both of you to have a check-up."

"I'm fine," Lisa insisted. "All I want is to get back to my family. Are they here?"

"Yes, they're keen to see you, they're at the pub. Are you sure you don't want to go with Nicky to the hospital?"

"Positive. I'm relieved it's all over. I don't think he's a well man. I believe it was the voices in his head, forcing him to do what he did, and no, that's not me excusing his actions. We were scared, both of us were, and who is to say what might have happened to us if you hadn't come along and saved us? But that's it, we've been saved, and we need to get on with our lives."

"You do, and we'll ensure you get back to your family and friends soon. I need to call an ambulance for Nicky first."

Nicky rubbed at her wrists and shook her head. "I wouldn't want to put anyone out. I can ask Violet to take me. It's just a precaution."

Sam smiled at the younger woman. "We'll see how you feel once we get you up on your feet."

Oliver helped Nicky to stand, and her legs promptly gave way beneath her. Sam took Nicky's other arm, and between them they managed to get her standing upright.

"See, I'm fine. Once I start walking there will be no stopping me."

"We'll take you back to the village and reassess the situation once you've had a chat with Violet. You'll need to check in with your husband, he was due to get on the road at four." Sam peeked at her watch; it was now three-thirty.

"Can I use your phone? Oh, hang on, I think my phone is still in the man's car."

"We'll sort that out for you. Do you know your husband's

number?"

"Er, no, not off the top of my head."

"Leave it with us. Let's get you two out of here and into the fresh air."

Sam linked arms with both women, and Oliver helped support Nicky on the other side. Emerging from the barn, Sam cringed. The ART commander was standing there, waiting to see her.

"Oops, I could be in trouble here. I'll be right back."

The commander moved towards her, his face contorted with anger. "What's the point in requesting we attend a scene if you have no intention of waiting for us before jumping the gun?"

"I'm sorry. Things developed quickly, and we didn't have time to hang around, we had to deal with the situation without putting more lives in danger. Sorry you've had a wasted trip."

He held her gaze, lifted his shoulders in a defeated shrug, turned his back and muttered, "Glad the outcome was a positive one and you didn't end up with a massive dose of egg on your face."

Sam grinned and watched him leave the driveway. "Where's Jim's car, Bob?"

"I spotted it around that side of the barn." He pointed to a smaller dilapidated building on the far side of the courtyard.

Sam wound her way towards it and opened the car door which was unlocked. There, lying in the footwell of the back seat, was a mobile which she took back to Nicky. "Is this it?"

Relieved, Nicky smiled and took the phone. "Yes, thank you so much."

"We'll give you some privacy."

Sam took Lisa back to her car and made her comfortable in the back seat. A tearful Nicky joined them a few minutes later.

"Everything all right?" Sam asked.

"Yes, I just caught him before he set off. He's ordered me to go to the hospital."

"I thought he might. We can drop you off on the way through, or ask Violet if she'll take you, whichever is easiest for you."

"I'm sure Violet wouldn't mind, then we can pack our bags and get on the road. It feels so good to be making plans again, knowing what might have happened if that crazy bastard…"

Sam rubbed her arm. "You're safe, that's all that matters. That and the health of your baby."

They drove back to the village to find Emma upstairs with Claire.

"Don't tell me off. I couldn't up and leave this place, not with everything that is going on," Emma said, her cheeks tinged with colour.

"All's well that ends well. We seized an opportunity to pounce on him without putting either of the women's lives in danger."

"Delighted you found them. Did he hurt either of them?"

"No, apart from Nicky having a punch to the stomach. She's on her way to hospital to get checked out as she's pregnant. So, that's our time over here now, Emma. The killer has been caught, thanks to you and your amazing staff."

"Not at all. You're being kind, we only pointed you in the right direction, you guys did all the hard work. Don't be a stranger, Sam. I've enjoyed the time we've spent together this week, even under such bizarre circumstances."

"You have my word that you'll be seeing plenty more of me in the future. I have no intention of letting the tragic events of what we've dealt with this week put me off the area."

EPILOGUE

*S*am wrote off her weekend to concentrate on getting the murder investigation locked down on Jim Kirk. It wasn't looking good, though, not since she'd had a private chat with Rhys. He'd advised her to seek the professional advice of a shrink, someone she wasn't involved with romantically, to get their take on what was going on with Kirk. In Rhys's opinion, the man was bonkers with a capital B or suffering from what could be clinically called auditory hallucinations. Or schizophrenia, as it used to be termed. Which meant Jim could hear the voices that others couldn't. So many of these conditions changed names over time, even though it still amounted to the same thing. Individuals who had lost their mind, weren't deemed responsible for their actions in the eyes of the law and would probably never stand trial as such, for the crimes they had committed. Although, they would spend the rest of their lives in a psychiatric hospital, just like a number of other high-profile notorious killers in the UK.

It was no form of justice, not really, for the families who had lost loved ones at Jim's hands, or The Toothless Serial

Killer, as he was now known, after spending several days behind bars, both in a holding cell at the station and on remand at the local prison.

Sam went home Sunday night exhausted, only to be confronted by Crystal waiting to discuss the final details for the funeral. Her sister, who was usually really easy-going, was worked up about something. Sam could tell the instant she laid eyes on her.

"What's up, sis?" Sam removed her shoes, squeezed past Crystal who was blocking her path in the hallway and went through to the kitchen.

"Oh, nothing, except you were supposed to get back to me about the song choice for the cremation... but, somehow it has conveniently slipped your mind."

Sam removed an open bottle of wine from the fridge and poured herself a glass. "Do you want one?"

"No, I'm driving."

"Don't be angry with me, love, not tonight. I've had a week from hell, featuring the Devil himself to track down. I've worked eight days straight, and here you are, I sense, about to lay into me. Why?"

"Why? Because I've arranged every other detail possible to do with Mum's funeral. All you had to do was sort out your preference of what songs you'd like to be played during the service, and you haven't even done that yet. I need to get the decision in by the morning for the order of service."

Sam pulled out a chair at the kitchen table and collapsed into it. She turned her glass by the stem, her gaze drifting over to the door. Rhys came into view behind Crystal. He raised an eyebrow and put his hands up, pleading with her to remain calm. She'd always got on well with her sister, but since taking over the role of designated funeral organiser, Crystal had become unbearable to live with.

"Please, I'm begging you, can't we leave this for now?

205

Otherwise, one of us is likely to say something that we're going to regret. I've been under the cosh all week, trying my utmost to keep a tight-knit community safe from a serial killer who has been giving us the slip. I can really do without coming home to this, you bullying me. I'm shattered beyond words, believe me."

Crystal sat opposite her, and Rhys took up a position behind Sam. He rested his hand on her shoulder, giving her the strength to proceed.

"I'm sorry," Crystal whispered. "I didn't ask for all of the arrangements to fall on me, it just happened that way, and now, over the last few days, I've been overwhelmed."

Sam reached across the table and patted her sister's hand. "I should be the one apologising. Why don't we go over things, while we've got five minutes spare? We're both after the same goal, aren't we? To give Mum the best send-off possible."

"What about you having a rest? I can come back tomorrow if you'd prefer?"

"No, let's get it over with. What choices have you narrowed it down to?" Sam asked.

Crystal gave her a list of twenty songs that she and their father had chosen.

"You honestly want my thoughts?"

"Doh! I'm guessing that's not the brightest thing you've said this week, love."

"Okay, how many do we need?"

"Three, one at the beginning of the service, one during the slideshow and, the final one while we're leaving the crematorium. The last one can be a quirky or funny one, the vicar said, within reason."

"This is what I would choose. 'Three Times a Lady' by the Commodores to start off the proceedings, 'Because You Loved Me' by Celine Dion to accompany the slideshow, and for the final song, what about something like 'Ring of Fire' by Johnny Cash? I know it's not on the list but…"

"I love that idea," Rhys said.

"I'm not sure. I'll need to run that one past Dad, but the other two are spot on. I think Mum would approve."

"I think she would, too."

Crystal requested the list and dropped it into her handbag, then stood. "See, that was pretty harmless, wasn't it? I'll run the choices past Dad and get back to you."

Sam walked her sister to the front door and shared the warmest of hugs.

"Sorry," Sam whispered. "I shouldn't have left it all to you to sort out."

"What's done is done. Love you, Sam, don't ever forget it."

"Ditto. Take care, sweetheart. Give me a call if anything goes to pot and you need a hand."

"You might regret saying that."

THE DAY of the funeral finally arrived. Sam and Rhys met up with Crystal, Vernon and their father at her parents' house. From there, the cortege made its way to the crematorium at Distington. There wasn't a dry eye in the house once 'Three Times a Lady' began playing, and Vernon and her father helped a couple of the pall bearers to carry the coffin. Sam, Crystal and their father all read out their relevant eulogies which included their mother's greatest accomplishments, plus a few funny anecdotes from their mother's life.

The crematorium was filled to the brim. Sam's mother had been a popular figure in the community over the years, and they all played their part in giving her mother the best sendoff possible.

The wake was held at a local pub, close to her parents'

home, one they'd used weekly for years. The spread the land-lord had put on was amazing.

Outside, over a glass of wine, the family shared a private moment together and raised a glass to their mother.

"To Mum. Another star is now shining brightly, guiding our way. Till we meet again," Sam said. She clinked her glass against her sister's and father's and hugged each of them tightly for longer than she had in a while. "I love you, Crystal and Dad, more than you'll ever know. We'll get through this... together."

THE END

THANK you for reading To Catch A Killer the next thrilling adventure **To Believe The Truth**

HAVE you read any of my other fast paced crime thrillers yet? Why not try the first book in the DI Sara Ramsey series <u>No Right to Kill</u>

OR GRAB the first book in the bestselling, award-winning, Justice series here, <u>Cruel Justice.</u>

OR THE FIRST book in the spin-off Justice Again series, <u>Gone In Seconds.</u>

. . .

PERHAPS YOU'D PREFER to try one of my other police procedural series, the DI Kayli Bright series which begins with <u>The Missing Children.</u>

OR MAYBE YOU'D enjoy the DI Sally Parker series set in Norfolk, <u>Wrong Place.</u>

OR MY GRITTY police procedural starring DI Nelson set in Manchester, <u>Torn Apart.</u>

OR MAYBE YOU'D like to try one of my successful psychological thrillers <u>She's Gone</u>, <u>I KNOW THE TRUTH</u> or <u>Shattered Lives.</u>

TO KEEP IN TOUCH WITH M A COMLEY

Pick up a FREE novella by signing up to my newsletter today.
https://BookHip.com/WBRTGW

BookBub
www.bookbub.com/authors/m-a-comley

Blog

http://melcomley.blogspot.com

Why not join my special Facebook group to take part in monthly giveaways.

Readers' Group

Printed in Great Britain
by Amazon

41832575R00126